"You look beautiful." Zach smiled.

"Why are you saying that to me?"

"Because it's true?"

April looked into his eyes. "Why did you come here tonight?"

Nothing like being direct. Zach took a step closer to her. "The thing is, I've tried not to think about you, but it's impossible. So I am officially giving up. I came here tonight because I wanted to be near you. To spend time with you and see if this is the worst idea I've ever had."

"And what idea would that be?"

"Would you like to go out for dinner sometime?" There. He'd asked her. Maybe the invitation wasn't as eloquent as he'd hoped it would be, but it was out there now. And it was up to her to accept it. Or reject it, but he wasn't going to think about that.

"Why?"

Okay, well, that wasn't the response he'd hoped for. "Why not? Isn't there som~~ething~~ on that second-chance li~~st~~ ~~we wanted to check~~s off together?"

Dear Reader,

I hope you've been enjoying Hope Center Stories as much as I have. Three different women on three different breast cancer journeys, but all of them strong survivors.

It's funny because though all three women are so different from one other, they each represent part of my own cancer story. In the first book, Sherri expressed my own thoughts and fears at the time I was diagnosed. With April's story, I was able to explore my own second-chance list of what I wanted to do after I was well again. Some of her items that she wants to check off are similar to those I had, but haven't completed as of yet. I need more of my inner April to come out and play!

This story is also about those caretakers who give up pieces of their lives to help family members. I was privileged enough to be caretaker to my dad before he passed away in 2008. I remember at times feeling so overwhelmed by his care that I called my mom to tell her I couldn't do it anymore. I couldn't watch as he faded away day after day. Yet looking back on it now, I wouldn't trade that time with him for anything. I grew closer to my dad and cherish those small moments we shared. While Zach might not yet appreciate his own struggles with caring for his mom, I hope to show that caretakers are indeed special and blessed.

Thank you for passing along these stories to family and friends. We are always stronger together!

Syndi

HEARTWARMING

Healing Hearts

———

Syndi Powell

❤HARLEQUIN® HEARTWARMING™

Recycling programs
for this product may
not exist in your area.

ISBN-13: 978-1-335-63351-4

Healing Hearts

Copyright © 2018 by Cynthia Powell

Printed in U.S.A.

HARLEQUIN®
www.Harlequin.com

Syndi Powell started writing stories when she was young and has made it a lifelong pursuit. She's been reading Harlequin romance novels since she was in her teens and is thrilled to be on the Harlequin team. She loves to connect with readers on Twitter, @syndipowell, or on her Facebook author page, Facebook.com/syndipowellauthor.

Books by Syndi Powell

Harlequin Heartwarming

Afraid to Lose Her
The Sweetheart Deal
Two-Part Harmony
Risk of Falling
The Reluctant Bachelor

Sometimes family isn't the one you're born into, but the one you create.

To my stepdad, Russell D'Hondt, who loves to come up with twists and turns in the plot with me (you can thank him for helping me out of many a writing corner!) and who treats my mother like the queen she is. And to my stepbrother, John D'Hondt, who is showing us all how to take charge of your own life and make a difference instead of excuses.
Keep up the great work!

CHAPTER ONE

APRIL SPRADER WANTED one moment of sanity. Just one minute when she didn't have to run between examination rooms because she didn't have enough staff, which she didn't. Her emergency department was shorthanded. Again. Half of the doctors and nurses out with the flu. Again. And the patients kept coming. She listened to her current patient's breathing sounds. "Another deep breath, please."

The older man sucked in air. She could hear the distinctive wheeze of infected bronchial tubes and removed the stethoscope from her ears. "I can run more tests, but it seems you have bronchitis."

The man had a scrunched expression. "Not pneumonia, then."

"Like I said, I could run more tests, but you're wheezing due to inflamed lungs. They don't have the liquid buildup of pneumonia." She made a note on his chart and took a prescription pad from the front pocket of her lab coat. "You need to drink plenty of fluids and get some rest." She wrote two prescriptions and ripped the slips from the pad before handing them to the man. "You can either fill these here at the hospital or take them to your local pharmacy. One's for an inhaler, the other for a stronger cough medicine. If things don't improve in a week, see your regular doctor."

He thanked her and stuffed the prescriptions in the front pocket of his flannel shirt. One down. Only twenty-two more or so to go before she could take fifteen minutes for herself.

She left the curtained area and returned to the pit, where she checked the charts of waiting patients. Her head nurse, Janet, had prioritized them in order of urgency, so she only had to grab the top one and walk away. Heart palpitations in curtain five. Yep, that would be a priority.

She pushed the curtain aside and double-checked the chart. "Antonio Johnson?" She glanced at the African American kid sitting on the hospital bed. He looked no more than eighteen, although his chart gave his age as twenty-two, so why was he having heart issues? The kid offered her a weak smile as she stepped forward. "What brings you to my ER tonight?"

"He complained of chest pain and passed out at practice today." A good-looking man with artfully messy dark hair in a charcoal-gray business suit and light blue tie, with a cell phone plastered to his ear, moved closer to Johnson. "I need to know. Is his football career over? Is it his heart?"

She raised her eyebrows at this. "And you are?"

"His agent." He then ignored her and spoke softly into his phone.

April tried not to roll her eyes at him and focused instead on Antonio. "What were you doing before you passed out?"

"We were trying a five-ten-five shuttle run, which I've done a million times. And when I hit the forty-yard line, things got fuzzy and the next thing I knew, I'm lying on the field and the coach is yelling at me to get up."

The only words she had understood were

that he'd passed out on a sports field. "A five-ten-five?"

"You know. It's a drill we run at practices. But this was a tryout." Antonio gave a one-shoulder shrug. "I've never had that happen before."

"Your…" She glanced briefly at the man hissing into the phone. Really? "Your agent mentioned chest pains?"

Antonio shook his head. "That was before. I felt fine. Well, dizzy but fine. But you know. So is it my heart, Doc?"

She removed her stethoscope from around her neck and used the earpieces before pressing the chest piece to his back. "Take a few deep breaths for me."

The kid complied, and she could hear normal breathing sounds. She then placed the chest piece over his heart. She could hear the rhythmic beating as well as a distinctive click. She removed the earpieces and placed the stethoscope around her neck once again. "Have you experienced these palpitations and chest pains before?"

"No, he's in perfect health. This has never happened before. Like we said."

April was taken aback at the agent and tried to keep her lip from curling. "I was asking Antonio. My patient." She turned back to the kid. "Has this ever happened before?"

The kid looked at his agent, then shifted back to her. "Maybe a couple times, but then it was okay. And I didn't pass out or nothing."

"You never told me about that."

Antonio shrugged off his agent's comment. "It didn't seem like a big deal. I could feel my heart beating out of my chest, but then it would calm down. Besides, I was in the middle of a workout and your heart is supposed to be pumping that hard." He focused on her. "Right?"

She gave a nod and made some notes on his chart. "I'd like to do some tests to be sure I understand what's going on with you."

The agent scoffed. "Tests? He needs to be back on the field before the coach starts wondering if he needs to find another receiver."

She didn't second-guess herself, getting into the agent's personal space and poking him in the chest. "Hey. Antonio needs to be sure that this isn't something more serious, something that could end his life, much less his career."

The man clenched his jaw, and she could see a steady heartbeat in his carotid artery. He narrowed his eyes at her. "Can I see you in private for a moment?"

The agent moved past her and she followed him, but she wasn't going to back down. She didn't care how handsome he was or how important he thought his client was, Antonio needed these tests to confirm what she suspected. The man studied her name tag. "Dr. Sprader, I'm sure you can understand the pressure that Antonio is under. He's a rookie who needs to prove himself. Any kind of issue before he signs with the team, and he's not likely to see a contract."

"And I'm sure you can understand that my number one concern is the health of your client. That should be yours, as well." She put her hand on the curtain to push it aside. The man put his hand on hers to still it. She turned toward him. "Don't touch me."

He removed his hand from hers. "What if we promise to go to his regular doctor...to-morrow?"

She doubted that they would make it a priority if Antonio had a tryout scheduled at the same time. "What if I order these tests, and you stop interfering with my job?"

"He's my job, too. My client."

"And he's my patient. Now, why don't you go to the cafeteria and get a coffee while I take care of Antonio?" She glanced down at his buzzing phone. The sound was annoying. "Or better yet, take your phone to the parking lot and look after your business so I can look after mine."

The agent bristled, but put his phone to his ear and stalked away. April seized a deep cleansing breath to center herself and focus again on Antonio. Now she pushed the curtain aside. "Okay, then. I'm ordering an echocardiogram to get a better picture of what's happening with your heart."

Antonio's face paled. "Doc, be straight. Is it bad? Am I going to die? Is my football career over already?"

"Let's see the results of the tests first, then I'll have a cardiologist take a look at you, too." She put a hand on his knee. "If it's what

I suspect it is, with treatment and observation, you'll still have a long life."

He gave a nod, then cocked his head to the side. "And football?"

"You can still have that, too." She made more notes on his chart. "But let's wait and find out what the tests say."

She sent him a reassuring smile and stepped beyond the curtain. As she did so, a man grabbed her and put a knife to her throat. "Where's the drug closet?"

Great. It was going to be one of those days.

ZACH HARRISON FINISHED his last phone call and glanced back at the entrance to the emergency room. Coach Petrullo had called to check on Antonio's condition. "The overzealous doctor is running tests, but Antonio will be on the field good as new tomorrow," he'd assured the man. He only hoped he hadn't overstated the truth. The kid had to be okay. He was young and active. His football career was about to begin. Fate wouldn't be so cruel as to take it away. Right?

Zach slipped his phone into his suit coat pocket and walked through the open automatic doors. He needed Antonio in action, but he needed the kid healthy even more. He regretted how callous he'd probably come across to Dr. Sprader earlier. He'd noticed how she'd barely kept her contempt under wraps, and he wanted to go back in time and change that. He wasn't that kind of guy. He could be nice. A sweetheart, even. Though he'd been accused of using that to his advantage, rather than being sincere.

Shaking off all thoughts of his ex-wife, he practiced what he was going to say to the cute doctor and headed toward where Antonio waited. He saw the doc talking to another patient, a man who seemed to be standing too close to her. Zach paused and assessed the situation. Not only was the guy standing too close, the knife in his hand meant he was a threat. Zach couldn't spot the security guard he'd seen earlier in the hallways. He knew what he had to do. He'd had self-defense training for situations like this.

He sauntered up to the curtained area. The patient noted him and waved the knife. "Stop. Or I'll slice her throat. I swear I will."

Zach held up his hands. "I'm not going to

stop you. I'm only here for my client." He pointed to Antonio, who watched with wide eyes. He looked as if he were ready to jump off the bed and pummel the guy. Zach waved him off. "Why don't you tell us what you want?"

The grizzled man wore clothes that smelled as if they hadn't been washed in weeks. "I want to stop the pain."

Dr. Sprader struggled in the guy's arms. "I told you last time that you don't need the drugs, Harley."

So the good doctor knew the man. Probably had a history of coming into the ER. Zach saw how Harley's grip on the knife was loosening the more they talked. His knuckles were no longer white from strain. Instead, he flexed his fingers on the handle. If Zach could keep them talking, maybe he could disarm the guy.

"Harley." The man turned to look at Zach. "What kind of drugs will help you? Maybe if you tell me, then I can go get them."

The doctor's eyes flared with emotion, probably anger and even shock. Harley licked his lips. "Oxy works best. Takes the edge off."

Antonio shifted in the bed, drawing Harley's attention to him. And as that happened, Zach rushed forward and did a roundhouse kick to knock the knife out of the guy's hand and send it skittering across the floor. Dr. Sprader used the man's shock to grab his arm and twist it behind his back. She pushed him facedown onto the hospital bed. "Go get security," she told Zach.

He nodded and ran to the front desk. When he returned, he saw that Dr. Sprader had help from a few nurses to keep the man subdued. The security guard came and took the guy away. Zach hurried to Antonio's side. "Are you okay?"

"Where did you learn a kick like that?"

Zach gave a shrug. "High school. I was a puny kid with a target on my back. Had to learn how to protect myself, so Pops took me to self-defense classes." He looked over at Dr. Sprader. "How about you? Are you okay?"

She gave a short nod as she reached up to touch the side of her neck. A small trickle of blood had stained the neckline of her pastel blue scrubs. She seemed to be barely containing what he figured was disgust. "Thanks for the assist."

Obviously, his heroics hadn't changed her first impression of him. "Any time." He turned to Antonio. "Let's start those tests and we'll find out what's going on with you, so that we can get out of here."

PAGE KOSINSKI, APRIL'S best friend, found her sitting on the floor of the women's restroom. April had hoped that she would have a few more moments of refuge before resuming her duties. Just another five minutes alone would have been great. Instead, she looked at Page, who had squatted down beside her and was checking the cut on her neck from Harley. "I told you that you needed to report him the last time he came here looking for drugs."

April slapped her friend's hand away. "It's no big deal. I'm fine. Harley got arrested and can now get the help he needs."

"But what if that guy hadn't been around to save your butt? What if Harley had really hurt you this time?" Page took a seat on the floor next to her. "You give people too many chances. When are you going to start putting yourself first?"

"Don't you think I've been sitting here asking myself the same thing?" She paused and asked Page, "Did you get a glance at my hero?"

Page waggled her eyebrows and waved her hand in front of her face. "Hot."

"He's also arrogant and too sure of himself." April winced as she got to her feet and stretched. "What am I doing here, anyway?"

"Working your shift like you always do."

April nodded. "Exactly. I told myself that when I defeated cancer, I would change. That I would go out there and do everything I've always wanted to." She held her hands out to her sides. "And what have I done? I'm back to working extra shifts and sleeping in the on-call room instead of going home. And why? Because it's more convenient to just stay here. I can't keep doing this."

"I've been telling you that for months." Page rose to her feet and washed her hands in the sink. She tugged a few paper towels from the dispenser and dried her fingers. She crushed the towels into a ball and tossed them in the trash can. "So what are you going to do?"

April peered into the mirror and stared at her reflection. She ran a hand through her curly hair. Before breast cancer had taken away her hair, it had been thin, straight and whitish blond. Now that it had grown back, it was honey-colored, coarse and curly. Sometimes she looked at herself and wondered where the woman she'd once been had gone, not just physically, but emotionally, as well. She had been bold. Sassy. And unflappable. Now she worried about everything. Self-doubt tied her hands and kept her stationary, rather than taking action and doing something. She gave herself a nod. "It's time."

Page raised her eyebrows at this. "Time for what?"

April turned and looked her squarely in the eye. "It's time to start living."

She pushed herself away from the sink and left the bathroom. Page dogged her at her heels. "You're talking about that second-chance list in your journal?"

"I've got my new body, so why not a new perspective?" She checked her cell phone and saw that she had four missed calls, two of them from her supervisor. She punched the number and glanced at Page. "Dinner later? Maybe call Sherri and see if she can leave Agent Hottie for the night and join us."

Page patted her shoulder and went briskly along the hallway to return to her own job. April's supervisor answered on the second ring. "Darryl, I'm fine. Just needed a few minutes."

"Well, get your butt back on the floor. We're swamped."

She bit her lip and took a deep breath. "About that. It's time we talked about the vacation time coming to me."

ZACH FOLLOWED THE aide who pushed Antonio in the wheelchair from the cardiology department back to the emergency room. The aide left them in a different curtained area from before, and Zach took a seat in a metal folding chair next to the bed where Antonio was now. Checking his phone, Zach saw several texts, many of them from clients and one from his mom's day nurse. She was asking him if he would be home at a reasonable hour, or should she arrange for an evening nurse to arrive before her shift was over. His fingers flew as he told her he'd call her once they left the hospital.

The curtain was drawn aside, and Dr. Sprader entered the cozy alcove. She looked different from before, though he couldn't put his finger on what it was. She wore the same pastel blue scrubs with the bloodstain on the collar. Her messy curls hadn't changed, and her face remained void of cosmetics. Not that she needed them. Her skin seemed to glow without any enhancement, and her blue eyes snapped with whatever thoughts danced in her head. She barely acknowledged him, before focusing on Antonio. "The results have come in, and I've consulted with Dr. Hall, a cardiologist on staff." She took a seat on the edge of the bed. "You have mitral valve prolapse."

Antonio clutched at his chest. Zach reached over and patted the boy's hand. "Doc, am I dying?"

She shook her head. "Your heart valve is leaky, which causes a murmur. Things like stress or overexertion will aggravate the situation, giving you palpitations and chest pain."

She passed several business cards to Antonio. "Here are a few cardiologists in the area. Choose one to follow up with. You're going to want a good one on your team, so I'd recommend Dr. Hall, but feel free to ask around for recommendations." She shifted her attention to him, and Zach tried not to stare. "Questions?"

Was she single? He doubted it. Women like her with beauty and smarts tended to be unavailable. He cleared his throat. "So he can keep playing, then?"

"With monitoring, medication and some lifestyle changes, there's no reason he can't live with this until the off-season. But then I'd recommend surgery at that point."

Antonio let out a loud "Yes!" He jumped off the bed and pulled her into a hug that nearly crushed her. "Thanks, Doc."

Then he and Antonio knocked knuckles in an elaborate handshake that Antonio made him learn the moment after the kid signed the contract to work with him. "We really dodged a bullet on this one, Zach."

Antonio turned back to the doctor. "So

I can go?" he asked. When she nodded, he walked out with hands raised high in triumph.

Dr. Sprader handed him some business cards. "He needs to follow up with a cardiologist, and I get the impression you're going to have to be the one to convince him. This isn't a dire condition, but he needs regular checkups so that things like collapsing on the field won't happen again."

"Understood." Zach shrugged back into his suit coat and put the cards in his inside pocket.

As he walked by her, she reached out and touched his coat sleeve. "About what happened with Harley earlier."

He turned to face her. He'd been waiting for this. "There's no need to thank me."

Her eyes narrowed. "I was going to tell you that it wasn't necessary. That I had things under control before you jumped in."

He pointed to her neck where the knife had cut her. "I can see that."

"Harley is harmless. He wouldn't have actually cut my throat." She glared at him. "I don't need a hero."

He raised an eyebrow. "Are you sure about that, Dr. Sprader?"

"Perfectly." She continued to stare at him and then exhaled. "You know my name, but I don't know yours."

He extended his hand. "Zach Harrison."

She put her hand in his and gave it a quick shake. "Make sure Antonio sees one of the cardiologists, Mr. Harrison. Otherwise, his career won't save him from another episode."

Zach's phone started buzzing. He gave a brisk nod, then left her, his phone already at his ear. She may be interesting, but he had other priorities right now.

APRIL PULLED UP in front of the house that belonged to her friends Sherri and Dez Jackson. While she would have liked an evening out, Sherri had been under the weather. April retracted the phrase. What Sherri felt…it was as if her body had been scorched to get the cancer out. April remembered the sensation and gave a shiver that had nothing to do with the snowflakes drifting down from the sky. Her days battling cancer were long over, thank goodness. Now she had to put her life back together, hopefully better than it was before. She needed balance between work and personal life. Correction. She needed to get a personal life.

She grabbed her purse and journal from the front seat and exited the car. Page pulled in behind her, so she waited for her to park. They walked up to the front door, unsure of how they'd find Sherri. April knocked and soon Agent Hottie answered the door. "She's in the family room," Dez told them after the perfunctory hugs and kisses. "And I don't need to tell you two to take it easy on her. Don't wear her out."

"We know how she's feeling better than you do." Page shoved a pizza box into his hands. "For you and Marcus to share. Us girls have our own."

They walked through the living room and kitchen and down one step where they found Sherri on the sofa with her legs up on the coffee table, wrapped in a fleece blanket. She looked up at them and gave a watery smile. "Thanks for bringing the girls' night to me."

She had dark shadows under her eyes and looked as if she could fall asleep at any moment. April put a hand on her shoulder. "If you're not up for company…"

"Don't you dare leave me." She pointed to two recliners adjacent to the sofa. "Now, sit and tell me something good."

"April got a knife pulled on her in the ER today," Page said, opening their box of pizza.

Sherri gasped. "And that was good?"

"Because of it, she met a hot guy who saved her by kicking the knife out of the junkie's hand." Page offered a slice of pizza to Sherri, who waved it away. She then handed the slice to April.

Sherri gave a soft smile. "And who was this hot guy?"

"An annoying jerk who wanted me to tell him his client was fine without running any tests." April took a bite of her pizza and chewed, thinking about Zach Harrison. "If he hadn't been so irritating, I might have found him attractive." Page and Sherri exchanged glances. April pointed between them. "What does that look mean?"

Page cocked her head to the side. "It means he's your soul mate, obviously."

What? That was the most ludicrous idea

she'd ever heard. She was about to tell them so when they burst out laughing.

Still chuckling, Sherri said, "She's joking. It means we're happy that you finally have started to notice men."

"I notice them." April paused when she saw Page roll her eyes. "I just choose not to do anything about it."

"And when is that going to change? I thought getting back in the dating scene was on your list." Page gestured at the journal that April had placed next to her chair. "Isn't that what you were talking about earlier? That it's time to begin living your life again? To start dating and falling in love."

"Yes, it's time." She opened the journal and found the page where she had written a second-chance list of things to do when she was healthy again. She'd pored over the list as she'd sat in the chair during chemotherapy. Written and rewritten it until she'd found the top twenty things she most wanted to do. Number four was to start dating. "So how do I do it?"

Page gestured at Sherri, who shook her head. "Don't look at me. Dez and I didn't really date before we got married. I mean, we'd been friends for years, but we didn't date."

"And I haven't exactly been single for that long." Page rubbed her left ring finger. The wedding band was removed a few weeks ago when the divorce became final. "There are plenty of online sites to help you find dates."

April made a face. "I'm not sure about that. Don't you two know anyone you can set me up with?"

Sherri snapped her fingers. "What about my cousin Mateo? He's single, and I guess he's good-looking."

She remembered meeting him last summer at a party celebrating Sherri's last chemo appointment. "He's not my type."

Page held up one hand like a stop sign. "Hot and available is not your type?"

Sherri turned to Page. "You think Mateo is hot?"

"So does every other woman in Detroit. Come on. The man is seriously good-looking." Page fanned herself. "And you want to pass that up, April?"

April gave a shrug. "All right. If he agrees, I guess I could go out with him."

Dez joined them and handed Sherri a cup of steaming tea that brought the scent of ginger with it. "You ladies all right out here?"

Sherri kissed his hand before taking the mug. "Dez, do you know any available guys for April?"

"I don't know. Maybe. What's your type, April?"

"It's been so long, single is her type." Page snapped her fingers. "There's that one doctor who asked you out a while ago, but you took no notice of him."

"Because I'd just been diagnosed with cancer. I wasn't worrying about dating at the time." She remembered how he'd stammered out an invitation to a concert. She could only think that she might be dying, and going to see a symphony was the least important thing she could do at the time. Figuring out how to survive had been her focus.

"Well, things have changed. What was his name again?"

"Dr. Sperry, and he got married this past summer." He'd even invited her to the wedding along with half of her staff. She'd declined but sent a gift.

"Oh."

"Besides, I don't want to date another doctor. My schedule is hectic as it is."

Sherri put down her phone, then smiled. "I gave Mateo your number, so don't be surprised if you hear from him."

Her stomach clenched, and she put her half-eaten slice of pizza back on the paper plate. "You really shouldn't have done that."

"Well, are you serious about doing the things on your list or are you only interested in talking about doing those things?" Page leaned forward and touched her knee. "You've been given a second chance at life, April. Are you going to sit and let it pass you by or are you going to reach out and grab the opportunity?"

She'd already let too many things go, rather than pursue them. Men she might have dated and fallen in love with. Jobs that she might have excelled at. Opportunities that never came around again. Enough was enough—she needed to do this. Standing, she declared, "I'm going for it."

CHAPTER TWO

APRIL STUDIED HERSELF in the full-length mirror and put a hand to her chest. After her reconstruction surgery, the doctor had put an implant in her unaffected right breast in order to make both match in size. She now had more cleavage than she'd had before her cancer diagnosis. The coral dress she'd chosen to wear had a scoop neckline that dipped down more than she would have liked. Afraid her scars would show, she found a floral scarf and looped that around her neck and tucked it into the collar to give her some coverage.

The doorbell rang, and she took one last glance at herself in the bedroom mirror. She'd changed because of cancer, but then she'd had to. Tonight was for taking back her life. And who knew what the future held.

She opened the front door and whistled at Mateo, who stood on the porch in an emerald green silk shirt and black pants. He looked like he was ready to dance. He gave a lop-sided grin. "You look pretty good yourself."

She adjusted the scarf. "Did you want to come in for a moment?"

He gave a nod before ducking inside. She took a deep breath before shutting the door and turning to face him. No dating for over two and a half years—long before cancer had dominated her thoughts and days—she put her nervousness down to that. It's not like this was a blind date with a stranger. She knew she could trust Sherri's cousin. Knew she could relax and have fun.

He glanced around the room, then his chocolate-brown eyes were back to her. "This is a nice place. Cozy."

"It is small, but it's close to the hospital. Since I spend most of my life there, it made sense to move into this neighborhood. I could even walk there if I had to. But late at night in this neighborhood, it's not the best idea." She bit her lip to keep from babbling.

Mateo nodded and let out a breath. "Sherri told me that she met you at the ER."

"She told me that you're a great lawyer."

He cast his eyes down and gave a shrug. "I

don't know about great." He raised his head to look at her. "Are you as nervous as I am?"

April laughed and put a hand to her belly. "Does it show?"

He took a step toward her. "Let's just agree that tonight is about becoming friends and going out to have a good time."

He was already playing the friend card? But she agreed. Not that she didn't appreciate his trying to defuse the tension. "Do you want to head out?"

He helped her shrug into her coat, then he opened the door, letting her leave the house first. Just like a gentleman. He waited on the second step of the porch while she locked the door and put the keys into her rose-gold clutch. He even held her elbow as they walked down the sidewalk to his car. He opened the passenger door for her and waited until she had folded her legs inside and secured her seat belt before he shut the door and ran around to the driver's side. He started the car, and silence fell between them as they drove to the club. After a few minutes, Mateo spoke. "My cousin mentioned you wanted to try salsa dancing. Why salsa?"

It was one of the things on her list, something she'd added after watching a reality show about dancing. "Because salsa dancers look like they're enjoying the life they've been given. Sherri told me that you were an expert."

He laughed at this. "If by expert she means that I've been dancing since I was eight, then yes, I guess I am."

"Any tips?"

"Let the music guide you and follow my lead."

It sounded easy enough. When they arrived at the club, Mateo took her elbow as they stepped inside and searched for a table. The beat of the music made April's feet twitch, wanting to go out on the dance floor before she had learned any of the moves. She reminded herself that learning to salsa dance would take more than a good song playing on the sound system. She took off her jacket and handed it to Mateo, who left to check their coats and order some drinks.

Shortly after, Mateo approached their table with two drinks in his hands, a beer for him and a margarita for her. He handed her the bright pink drink, then glanced at the empty dance floor before sitting down. "When do they start the dancing?"

She took a sip and shrugged. "The website said nine." She glanced at her watch. It was about a quarter past. "Maybe they're running late?"

"Or maybe they're waiting for someone to get things started." He smiled at her. "Want to give it a try?" She took a gulp of her raspberry margarita and jumped up. Mateo took her hand as they walked to the dance floor.

"Start on your left foot," he said and slipped his left hand in hers and his right on her back. He took a step forward as he nudged her backward. She took a step back with her left foot, then a step with her right and brought her left in line. Then he drew her forward a step. Her ankle wobbled on the heel of her shoe, and he gripped her tighter to keep her steady, and they stopped in place. "That's the basic step. You'll do fine."

April gave a nod and stared at her feet. She remembered taking ballet when she was six, but had only lasted a year before she found that she preferred different pursuits like performing experiments in the science lab or reading about the life cycle of the earthworm. She'd left sports and physical activities to her brother, Tony, until now. *Feel the beat*, she chanted to herself. *Follow Mateo's lead. Stop thinking and just feel.*

Mateo's gaze searched her eyes. "Ready to start again?"

"You bet." He nudged her backward again. This time, she stayed steady on her feet, switched off her brain for a few seconds while she followed his moves. Mateo grinned. "Now, I'm going to spin you. Ready?"

He held their hands up high, and she spun around under them. When she turned back to face him, she laughed. "I'm dancing."

He returned her smile. "Yes, you are." He tightened his grip on her hand. "Okay, now let's try a different step."

They started as they had before. Back, forward, then he put his arm around her shoulders and they danced side by side rather than facing each other. He spun her into their original position and started the sequence again. April whipped her head back on one of the turns and lost her footing again. Mateo caught her before she could hit the floor. "Sorry."

"Don't apologize. You're doing really well for your first time salsa dancing."

The song ended, and they headed to their table. April sipped her margarita and watched as other dancers filled the dance floor. The way they moved effortlessly and in sync amazed her. Even if she took dance lessons for six months, she doubted she could move as easily as the women dancing. She might dance better than tonight, but she'd still struggle with turning off her brain and letting her body take over.

She found Mateo watching her. "You look lost in thought," he said.

Story of her life. "Sherri said you're helping her and Dez finalize Marcus's adoption." The couple had planned on being his foster parents, but had recently taken steps to legally make him a part of their new family. "She's so happy."

"She deserves to be after all that she's going through." He watched her over the top of his beer glass. "And how are you feeling?"

Sherri had told him about her cancer? "Real

good." She sipped her drink, then motioned with her head to the dance floor. "Want to give it another try?"

"Okay, okay." He drained his beer, put his arm around her waist and led her to the dance floor.

After three songs, April's heart pounded, and a fine sweat had formed along her hairline. She let go of Mateo's hand and fanned herself as the song changed to something slower. He raised an eyebrow at her. While she longed to sit, her body had something different in mind and she took his outstretched hand in hers.

They danced, their bodies close. Touching, then he nudged her away and spun her around and brought her close to him again. It felt like a tug-of-war between the two of them, but one that Mateo controlled the entire song. The intimacy of the dance should have made her feel a stirring of emotion for the man holding her close, but she felt nothing. Friendship sure, but not that pull of attraction. At the end of the song, she returned to the table. Mateo left her to get glasses of water. She ran her hands through her curls in an attempt to cool herself. A guy in a suit stopped beside her. "Dr. Sprader, you looked good out there."

She looked up and recognized that sports agent. "Mr. Harrison. I'm surprised to see you here."

ZACH HAD BEEN surprised to see April on the dance floor, and with a boyfriend, no less. He tried to ignore the hollow feeling in his chest at that thought and pointed at a corner where a hot new talent on the baseball circuit sat with his girlfriend. "I brought a potential client tonight."

She glanced in the direction he'd indicated and frowned. "You dumped Antonio already?"

"I have more than one client. Just like you see more than one patient." He tried not to let her comment hit him hard, but it was too late. He got tired of being accused of having divided loyalties when he had to work for more than one client at a time. He needed to provide for his family, after all. And that didn't come cheap. He looked toward the bar where her date had disappeared. "You and your boyfriend dance really well together."

"He's not my boyfriend." She fidgeted with her purse, snapping it open and shut. "Not that it's any of your business, but it's our first date."

"Really? Based on how you were dancing, I'd figured you knew each other pretty well." He'd been impressed by how at ease she seemed after a few songs. They'd moved so naturally together that he assumed they were a couple.

A fast-tempo song started, and she stared out at the dance floor with a look on her face that made him wish he knew how to salsa. He wondered what it would be like to hold her in his arms and turn her around the room. Not that he had time for such frivolities as dancing. He needed to focus on his business.

Someone appeared next to him, and he turned to find her date standing there with two glasses of ice water. He handed her one, put the other on the table and offered his hand to Zach. "Thanks for keeping her company. You a friend of April's?"

She scoffed at this, and he shook his head.

"No. She took care of one of my clients." He accepted the date's hand. "You're a great dancer."

The guy gave a cockeyed grin. "My mother taught me when I was young."

"And he's a wonderful teacher, too." April put a hand on the date's arm and peered at Zach. "You don't want to leave your client alone too long."

Dismissed so quickly. Zach smiled. "You're right. I'm here for work, not for pleasure." He glanced at her again. "Good to see you, Dr. Sprader."

"Thank you, Mr. Harrison." She took a sip of her water. "Want to go back out there for the next dance?"

The date looked between them and gave a slow nod. "Sure. Whatever you want."

Zach shook the date's hand again and walked to the corner table. He took a seat next to his client, Chris Ramos. "Did you two discuss my proposal?"

Ramos put an arm across his girlfriend's shoulders. "Mr. Harrison, you've given us a lot to think about, but I'd like to get to know you a little more before I sign my life over to you."

"I can guarantee you that my terms are more than fair."

Ramos held up a hand. "Why don't we enjoy the music and dancing? There will be time for negotiating later."

Problem was Zach didn't know how to enjoy much beyond working and closing the deal. Just ask his ex-wife. "Of course."

The song changed and Ramos leaned over to his girlfriend to whisper in her ear. She nodded, and they left the table to join the dancers on the floor. Zach searched the crowd and found Dr. Sprader with her date. She looked fantastic in that soft orange dress and her dark blond hair wildly curling around her face. Her expression seemed to be lit up with joy as she turned in the guy's arms and swayed to the beat of the music.

He wondered what it would take to find a woman like her. And if he did find someone, if she would be interested in him.

He grimaced. He'd proved that he wasn't made for relationships. He'd failed miserably as a husband. He could provide financially, but not when it came to love and affection. He'd forgotten birthdays and special events. He missed anniversaries and holidays. Unless, of course, it was for a client. Those he remembered.

Dr. Sprader glanced in his direction and he looked away, self-conscious to be caught watching her on the dance floor. A waitress stopped by the table, and he welcomed the distraction to order another round of drinks. Ramos and his girlfriend returned to the table after a few songs. Chris gulped his beer and patted Zach on the back. "Man, this place is sick. How did you find out about it?"

"Came as a recommendation from a friend." Okay, so it was another client, but he didn't have many friends. He noticed that Dr. Sprader seemed to be leaving, her jacket over one arm and the other around her date.

Ramos followed his gaze and gave a small smile. "She a friend of yours?"

"No. We just met."

"For someone you don't know, you seem to watch her quite a bit." Ramos looked over at his girlfriend, who smirked and nodded. "She someone you want to get to know better?"

Zach turned his attention back to Ramos. The last thing he needed was to lose a client because his focus was elsewhere. "My life doesn't have much room for making new friends right now. I'm dedicated to my clients and their needs. I work tirelessly to get the best contracts and to make sure their lives are exactly what they want."

Ramos nudged him. "I get it. You'd work just as hard for me if I sign with you."

"So what is it that's keeping you from doing that?" Zach asked. He'd been wining and dining this guy for three months without a commitment. "What is it that you need? Tell me and I'll make it happen to get you on my roster."

Ramos and his girlfriend exchanged glances. He leaned in close to Zach. "We need to get married. And quick. You make that happen, and I'll be happy to join you."

Zach wanted to groan. Couldn't he have asked for something easy like playing for the number one team in the league at a cool six million a season? But he smiled and nodded. "Then you'd better be ready to walk down that aisle."

MATEO PARKED HIS car in front of her house and cut the engine. She peered through the window to concentrate on the porch light. Was Mateo expecting to come in? Would he kiss her or push for more? And did she want him to?

She licked her lips and shifted to face him. He kept his gaze straight ahead, focused on something in the dark. "Thanks for a fun evening, Mateo. I really enjoyed it."

He turned and smiled at her. "I did, too. More than I expected to." He winced. "I didn't mean that the way it sounded. You're nice, I mean, and very attractive. But…"

"But." She returned his smile. "It's okay. I liked our time together, but I don't feel that spark for you either. We'd be better off as friends."

"Right. Friends." Mateo let out a sigh. "I did notice some sparks between you and that guy who stopped at our table."

"Mr. Harrison? No, you're wrong. I've only seen him twice, and there's nothing there. Nothing. Not a thought or idea. Not a thing."

He stared at her with a faint smile on his

face. "Are you sure about that? You seem a little too adamant."

"I protest too much, in other words?" She gave a shrug. "There's something about him that really bugs me. I can't describe it."

She could tell Mateo wasn't convinced. Not that it should matter if he was. Mr. Harrison wasn't her type. She didn't want to get involved with a workaholic who spent his life on his cell phone, rather than paying attention to the world around him. She knew too well what that was like. And she didn't intend to go down that path again.

She gripped the door handle. "Thank you again for a lovely evening."

"My pleasure."

He started to open his door, but she put out a hand to stop him. "You don't need to walk me to the door. I'll be fine."

"I may not be interested in you romantically, but I haven't forgotten my manners."

She got out of the car and waited for him to join her on the sidewalk. At the house, Mateo stood on the bottom step as she unlocked the front door. When it opened, she turned and looked down at him. "Maybe I'll see you around."

"Good luck on your second-chance list."

"Sherri told you?"

He nodded. "I think it's great that you're trying to get back into life after your brush with cancer."

"It was more than a brush."

He frowned. "You know my mother died from breast cancer? It was horrible to watch the life drain away from her daily." His expression softened. "So the fact that you're grabbing life with both hands is something to be proud of. Best of luck with the rest of your list."

She stepped inside her house and watched him as he turned on his heel, got back into his car and left. She shut the door and locked it before placing her clutch on the table along with her keys. Leaning on the door for a moment, she retrieved her cell phone from the purse and texted Page. Salsa dancing fun. No sparks with Mateo.

A few seconds later, her cell phone rang. "What do you mean there were no sparks? The man is soooo hot, so smart—"

"We had a good time, but there was no chemistry between us." April plopped onto the sofa and kept the phone wedged between her ear and shoulder as she took off one shoe, then the other. "Besides, the cancer thing puts him off a little."

Silence on the other end. Then Page cleared her throat. "Did he actually say that?"

"No, he mentioned his mom died from it and how hard that was to watch." She massaged one foot and eased into the sofa. "It's fine. We'll just be friends. No big deal."

"So what's next on your list?"

She plucked her journal from the coffee table and opened it. "I saw an ad in the staff lounge about Italian cooking classes being offered nearby. You know I've always wanted to learn to cook, so why not pasta?"

"I don't think even you could burn water."

"Want to take the class with me?"

More silence, then a huff of resignation. "Fine. Let me know when and where."

ZACH BAGGED MRS. ZERELLI'S groceries as his grandmother rang up the purchases. "You've grown into a fine young man, Zachary."

"Thank you, Mrs. Zerelli." He tucked one paper bag under his arm and hoisted the second. "Why don't I walk these out to the car for you?"

She patted his cheeks as his grandmother beamed at him. "Such a *good* boy."

He escorted Mrs. Zerelli to her car and waited for her to unlock the trunk before placing her bags of groceries inside and slamming it shut. He waved away the dollar she tried to press into his hand. "It's all part of the Rossi service, Mrs. Zerelli."

Again, the woman patted his cheeks. "Francisco and Angelina are lucky to have you."

He swallowed the guilt that gnawed at him since he hadn't been with his grandparents much the last few weeks. But he smiled and opened the car door for Mrs. Zerelli, then closed it once she was inside. He waved as she backed out of the parking spot and left the lot.

Behind the register, Nonna was ringing the next customer's purchases. For a snowy Saturday in late February, his grandparents' market seemed to be bustling with business. Zach had planned on stopping in to get a recommendation for a caterer for the Ramos wedding, but seeing the lines and Nonna's stooped figure behind the register changed it. When he'd been a kid, he'd helped out plenty of afternoons and weekends.

He returned to Nonna's side and started to bag the groceries. She turned to him. "I'm surprised to see you. I thought you were at your office."

"It's Saturday."

Nonna gave him a look, and he flushed. Okay, so he'd been working a lot lately, but his mother depended on him. "Actually, I was hoping to get some ideas from you for a client of mine. Well, a potential client."

"I don't know anything about sports. You should talk to Pops about that. He's looking after the meat counter today." She told the customer the total cost of her purchases as he finished putting the items in the bags. "Have a great day, and we'll see you on your next visit."

The customer left, and Nonna started to ring up the next person's groceries. Zach leaned in to whisper in her ear. "This isn't about sports. It's about throwing a wedding."

Nonna paused from her work and stared at him. "I didn't even know you were dating."

He jerked up his hands like a criminal caught red-handed. "I'm not. Like I said, it's for a client. I need to throw him a quick wedding, and I know nothing about how to do it. The ceremony, the reception, caterers, music, Marissa took care of all of that before."

Nonna called over to one of her staff and had him take over the register. She put her arm through Zach's and pulled him into the office. She took a seat behind the desk, opened one of the drawers and brought out a large white binder. "These are all my neighborhood contacts. Flowers. Food. Music. A hall. Whatever you need."

Zach accepted the book and kissed her cheek. "You're the best."

She laughed and stood. "Now, out of my way. We're busy."

He glanced around the market. "I could give you a hand for a little bit."

"Trying to worm your way into a dinner invitation?"

He gave a shrug. "I haven't had your cooking in a long time. I think I'm overdue."

She paused. "And your mother?"

He didn't know what shape she'd be in, but

he could check on her and bring her with him if it was a good day. "We'll see."

"She's my daughter, and I haven't seen her in weeks."

Zach understood that, but his first concern was his mother's health. "Dinner at seven?"

This time, she kissed his cheek loudly. "You are a good boy."

He didn't know about that, but he tried. As he was leaving, he almost ran down a woman in a pastel pink jacket with matching hat and scarf. She tried to peer around him into the office. "Sorry, miss. Do you need something?"

She took off her hat, and he noticed that it was Dr. Sprader. Her jaw dropped at his presence, then she pursed her lips. "I was looking for Mrs. Rossi. I wanted to sign up for her cooking classes."

"It's you." He shook his head, knowing that didn't come out right. "My grandmother's right here." He turned to Nonna. "You still teach those?"

She shrugged and motioned for the doctor to come into the office. "I like to pass along my knowledge, so why not? Our next class is next Tuesday. Zach, it wouldn't hurt you to brush up on your cooking skills."

Dr. Sprader seemed a bit stunned. "Your grandmother?"

Nonna looked between him and the doctor. "You two know each other?"

"We keep bumping into each other." The doc bristled at that and turned her back to him. "I was hoping to sign up my friend and me. But I have to admit, we're both novices at cooking."

"I teach all skill levels. And if you're a beginner, all the better. You won't come into my class with awful habits. I can mold you." Nonna brought out a calendar. "And your names?"

"April Sprader and Page Kosinski."

Zach looked at her. She looked like an April. A woman with a spring attitude. Shaking off the dull grays of winter and embracing a rebirth. He gave himself a mental slap in the head. Where was he coming up with this stuff? "April." She faced him, and he realized he'd said her name out loud. "First dancing, now cooking. What are you trying to do? Mark off items on your bucket list?"

"As a matter of fact, yes, I am." She got out her wallet and handed Nonna a few twenties. "I look forward to our first class." She ignored him as she passed by him.

Nonna slid the money in an envelope and wrote the names on the front of it before securing it in one of the desk drawers. "You sure you don't want to come to one of my classes?"

"I don't have time to cook, Nonna."

"I figured you might want to join so it would give you an excuse to be around that woman."

He pointed in the direction April had left. "Dr. Sprader? I don't think so."

Nonna eyed him, but he didn't fidget or look away. "Something wrong with her?"

"Where do you want me to start?" He chuckled. "First off, she doesn't like me. Not that I'm all that fond of her."

"She seemed perfectly sweet to me."

He gave a shrug and clutched the book firmly. "Maybe, but I've got more important things to pursue. Thanks again for your contacts, Nonna."

"Class is Tuesday night at eight in case you change your mind."

But he wouldn't. He had a wedding to plan, a mother to care for, and clients who depended on him for their careers. The last thing he needed was a distraction of the female variety.

CHAPTER THREE

ZACH STARED OUT the window of his office, not paying attention to his cell phone. It buzzed with multiple text messages. He'd spent most of his weekend nailing down details for the Ramos wedding. He'd already downloaded the application for a marriage license and found a priest who would perform the ceremony at the banquet hall where Nonna knew the chef and had given him a discount since the happy couple would be married on a Sunday night. There were other details to take care of, but he'd made a sizable dent.

He pushed his wandering thoughts aside and picked up the phone. The first message was from Johnson, asking if he had heard anything yet about the offer from the Lions. Ramos wanted to know if they could fly out his parents from Puerto Rico in time for the wedding. And Coach Petrullo needed an update on Johnson's health. He answered them all. He'd make it work. Because that's what he did: took on the impossible and it happened.

His phone buzzed with a new text message. Bad day. Can you come home early?

He checked the time. Not even noon, and the day nurse wanted him to leave already? He replied that he'd stop by at lunchtime. He could kill two birds with that stone: get something to eat and check up on his mom. Then he'd drive out to the practice fields and talk to both Johnson and the coach. Life was all about multitasking.

He glanced out the window again, the gray February skies muddying his mood, turning it cold and dark. Images of Dr. Sprader crossed his mind, bringing a ray of sunshine to dissipate his gloomy state. Sure, she had appeared as if she were angry at him, but when he watched her with her patients, she had radiated something akin to kindness and compassion. A sort of contentment or…peace.

He straightened his tie and stood up. He didn't have time to think about what he didn't have. Better to focus on what he did.

He grabbed his wool trench coat from the hook behind his office door and stopped by his assistant's desk. "I'll be taking an early lunch today and stopping by practice to check on Antonio. Any messages before I leave?"

Dalvin huffed. "I keep this place a well-oiled machine. Nothing happens without you knowing."

Zach clapped Dalvin on the shoulder. "You've got my number in case anything does come up."

Dalvin pointed at his computer screen. "What do you think of these as wedding favors?"

Zach bent forward, scrunched his face. "We have to have favors, too?"

Dalvin shrugged. "I read about them on Pinterest." His assistant pulled several sheets and fanned through them. "These are all the wedding details that still need planning."

"That's why I have you." He sighed at the papers. "We'll review them when I return." He glanced at his watch. "Hopefully before four."

"You got it, boss."

Zach took the elevator to the parking garage below the building and walked to his sleek, black luxury SUV. Being an agent meant keeping up appearances, so he spent more than he should to project a successful image. He hit the key fob and unlocked the door before sliding into the leather seat and starting the powerful engine.

The drive from his office to his mother's house took about a half hour on a good day, but the recent snow had left the roads slushy, slowing drivers. He arrived at the house he'd grown up in and parked behind the day nurse's car. He took a deep breath before trudging up the snow-covered driveway to the back door. He unlocked it and jogged up a few steps into the kitchen. He turned right and found Dolores sitting at the dining room table, her head in her hands. She looked up at him when he called her name.

"Thank goodness you're here. She's been asking for you."

He raised an eyebrow at this and took his coat off, hanging it on the back of one of the four chairs. "She remembers me today? That's new."

"Well, she's been calling for your father, but she means you." Dolores stood and pulled the edges of her pink cardigan closer together.

"When I tried to explain that you're at work, she threw her cereal bowl at me."

He noted the dried milk spots on the cardigan. "You're a saint for putting up with all of this."

"And here I was thinking the same thing about you."

A shriek from the back bedroom caught his attention. He walked down the short hallway to his mother's room and opened the door. "Mother, I'm here."

Her blank eyes lacked focus as he stood in the doorway watching her. "I knew you'd come home," she said.

He stepped over clothes she'd probably thrown in a fit of temper and took a seat in the recliner next to her bed. "I always come home."

"Because you're a good man, Robert." She reached out and touched his cheek.

"I'm Zach. Your son." The doctor had said it was good to remind her of the reality despite her stubborn hold on the past. "Dad died when I was ten."

She blinked. "Zach." Her eyes searched his. "Zach should be home from school soon.

Such a well-behaved boy. Smart. Just like his father."

She put a hand on his, and he patted it before rising from the chair. "I'm just going to grab some lunch and then I have to go back to work, okay? But you be good for Dolores. She takes excellent care of you."

"I want you to stay." His mother pouted like a three-year-old who couldn't get her own way. "You promised you'd take me for a picnic."

"It's the end of February, Mom. We have to wait for the warmer weather." He noted the time and got a bottle of pills from the top of the dresser. Shaking out two pills into his hand, he said, "It's time for your medicine. This will help you feel better."

She took the pills like an obedient child, then fixed her gaze on the window. When she faced him again, he could tell he'd lost her once more. Her eyes looked at him, blank and confused. "I'm so tired."

He helped her lie back on the bed and covered her with the quilt Nonna had made. "I know." He kissed her forehead. "Why don't you take a nap? You always feel better after."

She snuggled into the covers and closed her eyes. "Wake me when Robert gets home."

"I will, Mother." He watched her for a moment, then left the room, quietly shutting the door behind him. He paused before continuing down the hallway. "She's taken her meds, Dolores, so she'll sleep for you." He shrugged into his coat. "Text me if you need anything."

"You can always calm her down. That's a gift."

He gave a nod, wishing he had the gift of restoring his mother's memory. That would have much more worth. From his car, he stared up at the house. He'd had to move in last year when his mother's condition had worsened. No longer able to care for her from a distance, he'd given up his apartment and most of his personal life to be the dutiful son.

And most days, he didn't regret it.

IN THE LARGE commercial kitchen, Page and April took their places at a stainless steel table where cooking utensils and fresh ingredients waited to be transformed into something edible. April wrinkled her nose as she picked up the recipe card. "Homemade pasta? Maybe we're not ready for this class."

"I got the night off to come here, so we're not chickening out." Page glanced around the kitchen as more students started to filter in. "Besides, I want to make this pasta so we can eat it. I'm starving."

"I told you to eat something before we came."

Page brushed off the suggestion. "I was feeling nauseous at the time, but I'm fine now."

April frowned at her friend. She'd been complaining more often about feeling sick lately. Considering it was Page, this wasn't unusual. The fact that she tried to downplay it was a concern, however. "Have you seen your oncologist lately?"

"Stop worrying about me. We're here to mark another item off your list."

Mrs. Rossi entered the kitchen, and the din of conversations among the students died down. She smiled at each of them. "I'm glad to see so many new faces mixed among my seasoned students. If you saw the recipe cards, you'll know we're making pasta tonight. It's an ambitious task for the first class, but you'll find that fresh pasta will make a big difference to your cooking." She picked up an apron and held it up in front of the students. "You'll find aprons below the table for your use, unless you'd rather go home sprinkled in flour."

April squatted down and found a stack of white aprons on the shelf. She grabbed two and handed one to Page. "You might want to get one more."

When April straightened, she found Mr. Harrison standing next to her. "You're taking the class?"

"My nonna thinks it will help me." He leaned down, got an apron and put it on over his head, covering the shirt and tie he wore. He wrapped the apron strings around him once and tied them together in the front. He looked natural with it on, and she found herself staring at him, her own apron still in her hand. He took it from her and slipped it on her, looking into her eyes as he secured the ties in front. "There. Now you look like a cook."

"Mr. Harrison—"

"It's Zach. And you're April."

Page waved her hand between them. "And I'm Page. You're the sports agent April has been talking about?"

April instantly glared at her. She hadn't been talking about him. Okay, so she'd mentioned him once or twice. And maybe she'd thought about him more than she should, but it wasn't like she was obsessed with him. "I told her how you subdued Harley in the ER."

"And how she saw you when she went dancing. And again when she signed up for this class." Page shrugged as April stared at her openmouthed. "What? Like it's any big secret?"

April gestured to Zach. "She makes it sound worse than it is. You'll find she's very good at that."

Mrs. Rossi came around and dropped a sifter on their table before tapping Zach's cheek. "I'd hoped you would come." She glanced at April. "But then I see you found a purpose to be here."

He glanced at April, then at his grandmother. "Thanks for that, Nonna."

Conversation stopped as they sifted together the all-purpose flour, semolina flour and salt into a large pile in front of the three of them. Zach used a fork to create a deep well in the center of the combined flours, and Page cracked open and added the eggs. Zach handed April the fork, and she started to mix the eggs together while Page put the olive oil into the mixture. When it came time to knead the dough, Zach rolled up his shirt-sleeves and did it like an expert. "My nonna had me knead a lot of dough as a kid. I've got this part down pat."

April watched the muscles of his arms as he pushed the dough away, then pulled it toward him, mixing it and forming it into a ball. She admired how his fingers deftly massaged the dough. Why was she thinking about his hands and arms? She didn't need Mr. Harrison... Zach to become a distraction for her. She was making her life better, and learning to cook was only the beginning.

Zach wrapped the dough in clear plastic wrap so that it could rest for a half hour. Attention returned to Mrs. Rossi as she explained how to prepare a basic pesto sauce. When she called for volunteers, April glanced around the kitchen rather than making eye contact. There was no way she was going to go up to the front of the class and show how inept she was at this. "Why don't we have April and Zach demonstrate what I'm talking about?"

Rats. Page sniggered behind one hand, and she gave her friend a look. Page shrugged and nudged her toward the front of the kitchen. April followed Zach to where two mortars and pestles sat on the kitchen counter alongside some ingredients: a leafy herb, bulbs of garlic and some kind of seed or nut. Mrs. Rossi had Zach peel and press the garlic while she roughly chopped the herb that turned out to be basil. "You don't want to shred it. Just chop it into smaller bunches to fit into the mortar and discard the stems."

Once they were done with that, Mrs. Rossi added some garlic and basil into each mortar, then had Zach and April pound the ingredients with the pestle. Mrs. Rossi tossed pine nuts into their mixture and had them keep pounding. Mrs. Rossi took the pestle from April and showed her a better technique to mix the ingredients into a paste. She wasn't surprised the older woman had such developed arms with the workout she was getting.

After the pounding, they spooned the paste into a bowl and included shredded Parmesan and olive oil to make a sauce. April leaned closer to the bowl and took an appreciative sniff. It smelled green and clean. Her tummy growled at the thought.

Mrs. Rossi dismissed April and Zach and demonstrated how to roll out the pasta dough and cut it into shapes. Page nudged April. "You looked good up there."

"Like I knew what I was doing?"

"Well, no. But you didn't completely embarrass yourself."

Page dusted the table with semolina flour and unwrapped the ball of dough. She placed it on the table, and April picked up the rolling pin. She moved the pin back and forth, frowning as the dough stuck to the pin. "What am I doing wrong?"

Zach put a hand on hers to stop her from tearing the dough. She almost dropped the rolling pin from the heat of his touch. "You want to move in several directions, not just back and forth. Let me show you." He put his hands on hers and directed them forward right, then backward left. Forward. Backward right. Diagonals and straight lines. The dough thinned and became smooth, stretching out in front of them in an oval. He sprinkled some semolina on the rolling pin, and together they stretched the dough out even farther.

Nonna stopped at their table and smiled. "This looks great. What pasta shape do you want to make?"

"Ravioli," Zach said. She patted his cheek and moved on to the next group. When Page and April looked at him, he shrugged. "I used to make them with her. It's one of my favorite memories." He handed April a knife. "You'll want to cut the pasta in squares of equal size."

She looked at the beautiful yellow dough in front of them. It was almost too pretty to cut into anything, but she carefully placed the knife on one edge and drew it down to the other. Once they had the dough cut into neat squares, Zach retrieved ricotta and Romano cheeses, eggs and parsley. He gave the parsley to Page to chop while April shredded the Romano cheese. He measured the ingredients into a silver mixing bowl, then showed them how to put a tablespoon of the cheese mixture in the middle of one square then place a second over it, pinching the edges to seal it up tight.

April stared at him. "I thought you couldn't cook?"

He leaned over one ravioli, pinching the edges. "Despite what my nonna believes, I do know how. I just don't have the time to do it." He placed the ravioli on the overflowing plate, then looked up at her. "Can you cook?"

She shook her head. "I can microwave frozen meals and chop vegetables for a salad. I also pour a mean bowl of cereal."

He grinned and brushed the tip of her nose. "You had a little flour there."

She reached up to where he'd touched her. "Is it gone?"

Page cleared her throat. "You're fine. So, Chef Boyardee, what do we do next?"

ZACH REALIZED HE'D been gazing into April's baby blue eyes for far too long. He glanced at her friend and gave a nod. "Right. Next step. We'll boil the ravioli for about six or seven minutes. Then we drain them and toss in the pesto."

"Sounds easy enough." Page took the plate up to the stoves where students had gathered to place their homemade pastas into the pots of boiling water.

With her friend gone, Zach looked over at April. She wore a soft sweater in a shade of blue that complemented her fair skin and eyes. It looked as if she'd be soft to the touch. Soft, vulnerable. What was he doing? He shouldn't be thinking about touching her. Yet, she seemed so approachable here in class. And that made her all the more appealing.

April started to gather the dirty dishes and utensils. He followed her to the sink, where he helped rinse them and place them in the dishwasher. They didn't say a word, but worked well as a team, then returned to their table. Nonna had left them clean plates and forks as well as a small mortar of pesto to try with their ravioli. "Your grandmother is amazing. I didn't know people could cook like this."

"This is nothing. You should see her at the holidays."

He rested against the table and watched

her. It must have made her uncomfortable because she sighed. "Do I have something else on my face?"

He shook his head. "No, no, you look beautiful, actually."

"What? Why are you saying that to me?"

"Because it's true?" He gave a shrug. "You seem different tonight."

She met his eyes and gave a short nod. "So do you. Less pushy and kinder." She looked over to where her friend Page waited for their pasta at the stoves. "Why did you come tonight?"

Nothing like being direct. He took a step closer to her. "Here's the thing. I've tried not to think about you. I've pushed you out of my thoughts so many times, but it's impossible. Therefore, I give up. I came here tonight because I wanted to be near you. To spend time with you and see if this other idea I had is my worst one yet."

She came up to him and stood toe to toe. "And what other idea would that be?"

"Would you like to go out for dinner sometime?" There. He'd asked her. Maybe it wasn't as eloquent as he'd hoped it would be, but it was out there now. And it was up to her to accept. Or reject, but he wasn't going to think about that.

"Why?"

Okay, so that wasn't the response he'd hoped for. "Why not? Isn't there something on that second-chance list we could cross off together?"

The friend returned to the table with their cooked ravioli. She thrust the ceramic bowl into Zach's hands, looked at him, paused, then she looked at April. "What did I miss?"

April shook her head. "Nothing. The pasta looks fantastic."

Zach spooned pesto on top of the ravioli, then flipped the bowl to toss them in the sauce. He spooned several ravioli on a plate and handed it to April with a fork. He did the same for Page, then he served himself. He watched April cut into a square, then place it on the fork and bring it to her mouth. She opened her lips and took a bite of it. He looked away only to find Page watching them as she chewed.

"Not bad." Page dug into the rest of her pasta.

April wiped the corners of her mouth with

a napkin and exhaled. "It's magnificent. And to think we made that from scratch."

He leaned in closer and dropped his voice so that only she could hear him. "We make a good team. Just think of what else we could do together."

April jerked back, crushing one of her friend's toes. She apologized, then put her half-eaten plate of pasta down. "I need to… I'll be right back."

Page frowned at him. "What are your intentions, exactly?"

He wasn't sure how much to tell Page. If April didn't want her friend to know what they'd discussed, then it would be better for him to stay silent. He shrugged. "Trying to get to know her better." He quickly added, "And you, too."

"Mmm-hmm." She narrowed her eyes at him. "Something tells me that she's the one you really want to know." She placed her empty plate on the table and came up close to him. "If you're playing games, she's not interested. She's been through too much to let a guy mess with her head. And if you hurt her, you'll deal with me."

"I don't plan on hurting anyone."

Page scowled at him, then looked in the direction April had just headed for. He all but dropped his plate of ravioli on the table, no longer hungry. He held up his hands. "Fine. I'll go talk to her."

He paused long enough to grab his wool trench coat before leaving the kitchen and walking to the parking lot. April paced, her arms across her body, shivering in the cold. He took several long strides to reach her, then removed his coat and slid it over her shoulders. "It's cold out here. You need a jacket."

She pulled the lapels of the coat closer around her. "Thanks. I wasn't thinking."

"What were you doing?"

She looked up at him and sighed. "Why did you ask me out?"

"I told you. I can't stop thinking about you. I figured it would be better to get to know you so I can have that time back to concentrate on my job." He noticed the snowflakes that had frosted her curly hair. He longed to reach up and brush them away. Instead, he crossed his arms over his chest and hunched his shoulders together. "Could we talk about this inside where it's warmer?"

April frowned at him for a few moments, then shook her head. "No, thank you."

"You won't talk to me inside?"

"No, I can't go out with you. I don't really like you, Mr. Harrison." She offered a polite smile, turned on her heel and presumably headed for the kitchen.

He had no choice but to follow, his curiosity piqued. He was a likable guy, right?

CHAPTER FOUR

FIVE WOMEN SHOWED up for the weekly breast cancer support group meeting at the Hope Center. April glanced at the other four women, one of them Lynn, the facilitator. "Where is Stephanie?" she asked as she took a seat in the circle.

Lynn winced as the other three women looked down at the ground. "She died over the weekend."

"Oh." Stephanie had been diagnosed with stage four breast cancer the same time that April had found the lump. She realized she'd been comparing the two of them at each stage of the disease, even though Stephanie's cancer had been more advanced. "But she seemed to be doing so well."

"Complications from pneumonia, they said."

Page entered the center and took a seat next to April, glancing at the somber faces surrounding her. "Who died?"

"Stephanie."

Page blew out a breath as she took off her coat. "Wow, I didn't expect you to say that. She was doing better, I thought."

Lynn nodded and took a seat, motioning the others to do the same. "That's why we should talk tonight about being vigilant when it comes to our health. How many of you thought you were healthy when you first discovered you had cancer?"

Nearly everyone raised her hand. Page sat on hers and shrugged. "I figured it would get me one day, so I wasn't really surprised. More like relieved that I could stop worrying about when it was going to happen. Now I could focus on getting it out."

"For the most part, we figured we were okay until our diagnoses. But our bodies had been sending clues that we probably chose to ignore or dismiss." Lynn sat forward in her chair. "I didn't do monthly self-exams because no one in my family had ever had cancer. Diabetes and heart disease, sure. But cancer? I assumed I was safe."

One of the women nodded. "I did my self-exams, but my cancer was too small to feel. So I thought I was okay, too."

"Now that we've had cancer, we need to listen to our bodies even more. If something doesn't feel right, have it checked out. Keep a journal. Talk to your doctor." Lynn glanced around the circle, her gaze landing on April. "Just because you've had cancer doesn't make you immune from everything else out there. Because you're a cancer survivor doesn't mean you won't have a heart attack, or like Stephanie, die from complications with pneumonia. Being a survivor means that you faced down one demon, but we still need to be on the lookout for others."

It made sense to April that having cancer didn't give her a free pass on other potential health issues. Though in fairness, it seemed as if it should. She'd had to go through so much already that she shouldn't have to worry about anything else. The reoccurrence of cancer was enough to keep her awake at night.

Lynn moved on to the sharing portion of the meeting, and one of the others talked about her recent scans. April noticed Page wasn't even pretending to be listening but picking at one of her cuticles. April leaned toward her. "What's going on?"

Page put her finger to her mouth. "Shh, it's sharing time."

Lynn turned to Page. "Did you want to share something with the group?"

Page shook her head. "Naw, I'm good for this week."

Lynn looked at April. "How are you coming along with your second-chance list?"

The entire group knew about April's list and had even brainstormed ideas to add to it. She shrugged. "We took a cooking class a few days ago. That was pretty cool."

"Tell them about the hot guy."

April frowned at Page. "The hot guy has nothing to do with my list."

"So you admit that you're attracted to him? Why won't you go out with him?"

"Because I don't like him. Sure, he's good-looking, but he rubs me the wrong way." April crossed her arms over her chest. "Why should I go out with someone like that?"

"You don't know him well enough to not like him." Page appealed to the group. "You should have seen the sparks between them when they rolled out the pasta dough."

Lynn's eyebrows shot up. "He asked you out?"

"Yes, and I shot him down."

"Isn't the point of your second-chance list to take you out of your comfort zone and see what else is out there?" Lynn pleaded, "Isn't going out on one date with him part of that?"

April bit her lip. Part of her resented Page for bringing up Zach. Another part knew she and Lynn were right. April hadn't given him a chance, but then why should she? If cancer had taught her anything it was that life was too short to waste on regrets. She couldn't explain why she didn't like Zach, but then, she didn't need to. She knew she'd regret it if she tried to get close to him. "No. My second-chance list is about doing things I've wanted to do but didn't have time for or the opportunity to pursue. It's not about squandering time with pushy men who have a cell phone stuck to their ear."

"Okay, okay. What's next on your list?"

"I haven't decided." She hadn't thought that far ahead yet. She figured she'd close her eyes and point to one.

"Wait." Page sat up straighter in her chair. "There's a doctor at the hospital that has tickets for an exclusive wine tasting. I couldn't go with him, so I gave him your number."

April groaned. "A blind date? Really?"

"Not so blind. You know Dr. Ross in Pediatrics?"

April glared and mentally scanned the staff at the hospital. "The name is familiar. Maybe I know him."

"Well, don't be surprised when he calls you. He definitely remembered who you were and seemed interested." Page gave her a bright smile. "And I know that going to a wine tasting is on your list."

It wouldn't hurt to give Dr. Ross a shot. But then why wouldn't she do the same for Zach? asked a little voice. She shook her head. Because that was a completely different situation. She'd seen Zach in action and hadn't cared for him. But Dr. Ross was a mystery. One she'd be interested in unraveling given the chance.

THE KNOCKING ON his bedroom door wouldn't stop. Zach checked the clock. A little after three in the morning. Rubbing his eyes, he walked to the door and opened it. "What's wrong, Mom?"

"You're going to be late for school." She peered behind him into the darkened room. "Why aren't you dressed?"

"It's not morning yet, Mom. And I haven't been in school for more than a dozen years." He put his arm around her shoulders. "Why don't you go on back to bed and I'll read you a chapter from your book?"

She smiled. "The romance one? Love stories are my favorite."

He nodded and led her down the hall toward her bedroom. "I know." He squinted from the bright light in the room, but helped his mom into bed. He sat in the recliner and pulled the book they'd been reading the past week from the bookshelf and flipped to where they'd left off earlier that evening.

As he read aloud to her about the Duke of Montmorency and the governess who taught his young ward, the words lulled his mother to sleep. After three pages, her eyes closed and soft snores accompanied his reading. He put the bookmark in place and watched her for a moment. When she slept like this, he remembered how she used to be—so vibrant, full of laughter and funny stories. Her eyes were clear and bright, not clouded with confusion. He missed his mother, grieved for her even though she was still alive. He wished he could do more for her, that he could find a doctor who'd be able to bring her back to him, restore the person she'd once been. Unfortunately, the doctors had told him her disease wouldn't get better. She had moments of lucidity, but they came less often. And she stubbornly held on to the past as her present.

He replaced the book on the shelf, then stood and covered his mother with the blanket. She stirred, and he held his breath to see if she'd stay asleep. Her eyes remained closed, so he leaned down and kissed her forehead. "Good night, Mom."

He tiptoed out of the room and turned off the light before slowly shutting the door. The snores on the other side meant that he could return to his own bed. But when he lay down under the sheets, he stared at the ceiling, unable to stop the tumble of thoughts in his brain. His mother's condition seemed to be getting worse. She'd soon need more care than what he could provide. And that meant finding a facility for her. He shut his eyes tight. He couldn't think about that now. Wouldn't try to imagine what it would be like to give up on his mother when she needed him the most.

April's face popped into his mind. The thought of her made him smile despite the fact that she'd rejected him. That was okay. He could ask her out again. There was something about her that intrigued him. That called out to him in a moment like this when he needed to be calm, when sleep wasn't coming.

APRIL FELT ALONG the sides of the teen boy's throat before she turned to the mother, who clearly fretted as she watched. "His glands are swollen, so it's probably strep throat." She took a tongue depressor and cotton swab from her coat pocket as well as the small flashlight. "Wade, I need you to open your mouth as wide as you can. I have to run a test to make sure what we're dealing with."

The boy opened his mouth, and she used the tongue depressor to stabilize his tongue while she ran the cotton swab along the red, inflamed tissues near the back of his throat. When she finished, she put the swab in a plastic tube and marked the sticker on the outside with Wade's name and hers. "I'll have the lab check this ASAP. When is the last time you visited your regular doctor?"

The mother gave a shrug. Based on the shabbiness of her winter coat and the scant information on the intake forms, April could guess that it had been a long time. The only reason that they'd shown up in her ER that morning was because Wade had stopped breathing in class when his throat had swollen to the point of closing. A quick-thinking school nurse had gotten him breathing again before the ambulance arrived. "If it's strep, I'll give you some antibiotics and you'll be off school for a few days until you're better." She turned to the mother. "Any questions for me?"

"How much will all this cost? I'm already missing work to be here."

"I'll get our information on payment plans, and the hospital can make arrangements with you. I'll be right back." She stepped out of the curtained area and almost ran into a tall man in a white lab coat with green eyes and graying temples. "Sorry, Doctor."

"Dr. Sprader? April, right?"

She nodded and tried to recall if she knew him. His name didn't register. "Did I call you for a consult?" It had been one of those days and she might have forgotten about it.

"I've been meaning to call you all week, but things kept coming up."

A lightbulb flashed on in her mind. "Dr. Ross and the wine tasting."

"Page told you about me? Good." He glanced around the crowded emergency room. "Do you have a few minutes for us to talk?"

She held up the tube with Wade's throat culture. "Gotta get this to the lab. We can talk while we walk."

She started to zip around patients and medical staff. The sooner she got the swab to the lab, the sooner she'd have answers for Wade and his mother. And she didn't want to wait too long and have other lab tests get in the queue ahead of her.

She glanced back once to make sure that Dr. Ross had kept pace with her. He was far-ing not too badly, only one or two people behind her. She paused as she got to the laboratory. He came up beside her. "You move fast for such a tiny thing."

She ignored the way the comment made her bristle. "You'd be surprised how often that skill comes in handy." And she strode faster through the laboratory's glass door.

"Dr. Sprader. April. Are you free tomorrow evening about seven?" he called after her.

She smiled at Javier, the intake manager, who accepted the swab and input the patient's name and date of birth in the computer. He smiled back. "We're about thirty minutes behind today."

April put her hand on his arm. "But you'll put mine at the top of the list, right?"

He winked at her and passed the throat culture to one of the lab techs. April turned to Dr. Ross. "You were asking me about tomorrow night?"

He frowned sharply. "Do you always flirt with the staff to get your tests moved up in the queue?"

"No. Sometimes I bribe them with cookies." She laughed at his dour expression. "That's a joke. Javier and his team follow protocol, so you can erase those frown lines on your forehead. I'll have my results in due course."

"Oh." He took a deep breath, then squared his shoulders. "Would you like to accompany me to a wine tasting tomorrow night? I've got tickets to an exclusive party, and your friend Page thought you might be interested."

She eyed him up and down. He wasn't bad-looking in an older, distinguished-man kind of way. He might lack a sense of humor, but then, she couldn't have everything, right? Learning about different wines was on her second-chance list, so she agreed. "Okay. It's a date."

He gave a brief smile and walked away. April discovered Javier watching Dr. Ross's departure. "You're sure about going out with that guy?" he asked.

She shrugged. "You're married. What other choice do I have?"

They shared a grin, and she pushed off the wall and zigzagged back to the emergency room.

ZACH FOUND AN empty parking spot behind Marissa's wine shop and checked his appearance in the rearview mirror before getting out of the car. Not that he needed to look good for her anymore. She'd made it clear when they got divorced that she had no plans for reconciliation. In fact, she remarried within a year and seemed happier with Jeff than she had with him. He tried to be happy for her.

He hit his key fob to lock the car doors, then headed along the alley to reach the street, turn and enter the wine shop, Metro Wines. He still had his hand on the doorknob when he was stopped by a tall man with a goatee. "Do you have your ticket, sir?"

He closed the door quickly to keep the cold air out and patted his coat pockets. Holding his hands out, empty, he replied, "To shop in a wine store? No."

"We're not open to the public this evening." The man started to edge Zach back to the door.

"Leo, it's okay. He's welcome to come in." His ex-wife sashayed toward them and opened her arms to him. He gave her a brief hug as she air-kissed him on each cheek. "I wasn't expecting to see you tonight, Zach."

"You didn't return my calls. If you had, you

would have known that I was coming." He whistled at the well-dressed clientele. "You're coming up in the world, Mare."

She rolled her eyes at the old nickname. "I'm hosting an exclusive, invitation-only wine tasting. Part of Jeff's marketing strategy to take Metro Wines to the next level."

Zach nodded. "Well, I'm here to get advice on wines myself. I'm throwing a wedding for one of my clients and need a few suggestions."

"It's always about a client."

"You know me so well."

She gaped. "You're welcome to stay, of course. I'll be introducing some new labels as well as recommendations of my favorites."

"Thanks." He waved to Leo, who still scowled at him. "Guess I've got a ticket, after all."

He strolled past the gatekeeper and took note of certain labels and types of wine. He knew only the basics thanks to Marissa's influence while they were married, and he wasn't much of a drinker. Only socially when he was out with clients, and then he tended to stick to the same drink: single malt whiskey probably due to his father's influence rather than his mother's Italian one. But he doubted that Chris would want a whiskey bar. Wine seemed to be more appropriate for a wedding.

A small figure in a very bulky pink parka barreled into the store and gave her name to Leo. He gestured her inside and Zach walked up to April. "Fancy seeing you again."

She took off her hat with the ridiculously large pompom on top and frowned at him. "What are you doing here?"

"Same thing you are. Trying out some wines." She scanned the room and her shoulders sagged. Zach followed her gaze. "Your date not here yet?"

"He called earlier to say he was running late and would meet me here, but I have a feeling that he's not showing up. We didn't exactly hit it off."

"There's still time, so, don't give up hope." Why was he trying to convince her that her date would be there? Maybe because she looked nervous, and she didn't deserve to be stood up. He whispered close, "Blind date?"

She shook her head. "No. Well, sort of. Maybe." She peeled off her coat and balanced it over her arm. "I met him once at the hospital."

"Another doctor?"

She nodded and looked him up and down. "You're here on a date?"

"No! No way, nope, uh-uh. This is my ex-wife's shop, although I snuck in without an invitation. Or date." He sighed. "We could have come together if you had agreed to go out with me."

"Not happening." She walked away from him and started to browse through the aisles.

Marissa stood at the front of the room and tapped a long, manicured nail against a wineglass. "Welcome, everyone. I have seven different wines that we'll be trying tonight. Paper and pencils are at each station so you can write down your impressions of each. And I have buckets for you to spit into after you've tasted the wine."

April grimaced horribly at Zach, who laughed at her shocked expression. "We spit the wine out? That's disgusting."

"It's part of the tasting experience. Unless you plan on getting completely blitzed, you might consider it."

"You know about wine tasting?"

He shrugged. "Only what Marissa taught me while we were married. But it's enough to get by on."

"Let me guess. You're more a beer kind of guy."

"You don't know me at all." He took the glass of white wine from a server who handed one to April, as well.

Marissa droned on about fruity notes and woody finishes. He sniffed the wine and nodded. "Not bad."

"You haven't tasted it yet."

"The smell, or bouquet in wine speak, is half of the wine-tasting experience." He held his glass to his nose and took a deep sniff. "You can smell the pear."

April mimicked his action and smiled. "I smell the pear...and something else. Some kind of spice."

"Not bad for a newbie." He took a sip and swished the wine around his tongue, then leaned over one of the silver buckets on the nearest table and spit out the wine. "I like this one."

April took a sip but swallowed it. "It's not

too wine-y." She giggled and covered her mouth. "I didn't mean it like that. I meant to say it doesn't taste so sour."

"If you're drinking sour wine, you're buying the wrong stuff."

"Probably."

She had a longer drink from the glass before Zach pushed the goblet away from her mouth. "Slow down there, Sparky. We have six more wines to go."

"Sparky?"

The door to the shop suddenly opened, and they both turned to see who was there. April shook her head when it didn't appear to be her date. "I'm telling you, he's standing me up. I don't think he really wanted to invite me in the first place. It was Page's idea."

"Well, he doesn't know what he's missing because you're great."

THE SERVER HANDED April another glass of pink wine, but she took it without really noticing it. She peered at Zach, his words seemingly hanging in the air between them. He thought she was great? She took a slug of wine without sniffing it or letting it swirl as some people were. And she definitely swallowed it, trying to figure out this puzzling man. "You really think I'm great?"

Zach nodded and sniffed the wine before sipping. "This is nice. I'll order a few boxes of this." He wrote the name on a slip of paper.

She couldn't keep track of the conversation. "Let's go back to your saying I'm great. You don't even know me."

"Something I've been trying to remedy, if you recall. I asked you out so we could get to know each other better." He put the half-full glass of wine on a nearby table. "I think you're amazing. And that's based on the very little I do know. You're an ER doctor. You're working on a second-chance list. And you're not afraid to try new things. That makes you pretty cool."

She placed her empty glass of wine next to his half-full one. "I thought you thought I was annoying."

"I never said annoying. You were pushy." He smiled warmly, and she lost herself momentarily to his charms. "You're not going to hold our first meeting against me forever, are you?"

The third glass of wine was pressed into her hand. She appreciated the deep red color, then buried her nose in the glass, smelling the currants and spices. She took a very small sip. That last glass of wine had been a wallop. She wrinkled her nose and put the glass down before finishing it. Zach smirked. "You're not a fan of the red?"

"Too heavy." Pushing the sleeves of her sweater up her arms, she asked, "Is it warm in here all of a sudden?" She fanned her face. "I'm having a hot flash."

"You're too young for those."

"Not when you're on the cancer meds I'm on." When he looked at her questioningly, she shrugged. "I take them to keep the breast cancer from coming back."

"Oh. I didn't know you had…" His gaze dipped briefly to her chest before returning to her face. He finished the rest of his wine and placed the empty glass next to the others. "Are you better now?"

"Yes. It's why I'm working on my second-chance list. Facing cancer showed me that life is fleeting. I didn't want to waste the rest of my life talking about doing things, rather than doing them."

"Makes sense."

"So now there's another fact for your file on me." She turned in Marissa's direction as the wine shop owner introduced the next bottle they would be trying. April turned back to Zach. "Now, you tell me one about you."

The server handed them each another glass. They sniffed, swirled and tasted. April made a face and shook her head as she placed the glass on the table. "No, I'm definitely not a fan of the red wines."

"My dad died when I was ten."

She stopped at the whispered confession. "Wow, I'm so sorry. That must have been hard on a kid your age. Any brothers or sisters?"

"Only child. Too bad. It's just been me and my mom for a very long time."

Her heart broke a little for the boy who'd lost his father. She couldn't imagine not having her parents in her life. Sure, they lived up north, about a five-hour drive away. But they were close, especially her and her mom. They spoke on the phone every Thursday night and texted each other during every episode of *Dancing with the Stars*, giving their own critiques for each dance. And her dad made sure to visit at the beginning of every season to make sure her gutters were cleaned or her furnace winterized or a million other little things she never remembered, but he did. The thought of losing them made her tear up. "No wonder you can be a jerk. You didn't have a father figure."

She bit her lip. Okay, she hadn't meant for it to come out like that. She tried to back up. "I mean, it makes sense that you can be so cold and distant." She winced. How awful was she? "That's not what I'm trying to say. Can you help me out here?"

Zach grinned. "Why? You're doing so well on your own." He took the next glass of wine from the server and handed one to April. "And I did have a father figure. My grandfather Francisco was a strong presence in my life. So you can't blame my coldness and distance on him."

"I didn't mean…" She glanced at the glass of wine. "I think it's the wine. It's making me say my thoughts out loud."

"Alcohol can do that."

"But I don't want to say them." She sipped her wine, a white this time, and beamed. "Yep, I'm a white wine girl. But I like mine sweeter than this. What about you?"

"I'm not a big connoisseur myself, but I don't like the sweet wines much. I prefer a dry red, full of body."

April shivered at the thought. "We're definite opposites, then." She let out a breath and glanced about the room, which had taken on a softness around its edges. The front door opened, and she looked again, but it wasn't Dr. Ross. He'd definitely ditched her. Maybe he'd gotten called by a patient? But she had a feeling it was more to do with her. Oh, well. Like Zach said, it was his loss. She was having a great time.

She paused. She was having a great time with Zach Harrison. There had to be something wrong with this notion. She didn't like him, but seeing him in this way made her earlier reasons invalid. In fact, she had felt sympathy for him. She closed her eyes. Had to be the wine, she told herself.

When she opened her eyes, she found he

was watching her. "Is your mother with you tonight?"

He seemed a bit shocked. "She's not here. Why are you asking?"

"Well, you said your dad had passed away and that it was only you and your mom. So, where is she?"

"Tonight, she's at home." He glanced at his watch. "Probably asleep with the television on."

"Does she live near here?"

"I'm living with her right now. She's had some health issues. I moved in to help care for her."

Why did he have to go and say that? Was he purposely trying to show her he was a nice guy? She groaned. "Next, you'll tell me that you donate to charity and play with puppies in your free time."

He peered at her. "Are you feeling okay?"

He put his hand on her arm, and she didn't protest or push it away. If anything, it felt like a comfort, an anchor. It made the room spin less, at least. She opened her mouth to tell him she was fine, but her stomach rebelled at having too much alcohol and no food. She turned to find the bathroom and instead threw up all over Zach's expensive-looking shoes.

CHAPTER FIVE

ZACH WAITED OUTSIDE the restroom for April to return. He glanced at his shoes and shrugged. They'd never been his favorite anyway. He'd cleaned them as best he could, but figured that the acid would probably leave permanent marks.

The restroom door opened and April popped her head out. "Is everyone gone yet?"

"No, they're still trying more wines. But if you want to make an escape, I can smuggle you out the back door." He pointed to the opposite end of the hallway. "My car is parked out there, and I can drive you home."

She shook her head. "I couldn't ask you to do that. Not after I ruined your shoes."

"You're not in any condition to drive yourself."

She brightened at this. "I didn't drive. I live not far from here, so I walked over. I can walk home. I'll be fine. I'm feeling better."

"No, please, I insist on driving you." There's no way he could let her walk alone in the dark while she was this tipsy. If he did, his grandfather would be disappointed in his behavior. Gentlemen made sure their ladies returned home safely. Even if April wasn't his lady, he still felt responsible.

He started down the hallway, but she tugged at his arm. "I left my coat in the main room. I don't think I can show my face there again."

"I'll go get it." He left her and returned to the store.

Marissa approached him as he grabbed April's coat from where she'd placed it on top of a display. "How's your friend doing?"

"She hadn't eaten anything since lunch, so the wine went straight to her head," he explained. "I'll be by tomorrow to pick out some wines."

"Promises, promises." She sauntered away, and he remembered why he hadn't been heartbroken when she'd left him. The woman could hold a grudge and remind him every day word for word why she did.

When he got back to the hallway, April was

half leaning, half slouching against the wall with her eyes closed. He put a hand on her shoulder. "You ready to go home?"

She opened one eye and looked at him. "Will you hate me if I throw up in your car?"

He winced as he put an arm around her waist and helped her take a few steps. "Maybe you could give me enough warning for me to pull over first."

"I'll try." She rested her head on his shoulder, and he tried to ignore the delicious way her hair smelled. Like flowers in a field on a summer day.

He held on to her as he opened the back door with one hand, then kept it open with his body as she slowly exited the store. His SUV was parked close by, so he hit the fob to unlock it and helped her ease into it before slamming the door shut and running around to the driver's side.

He started the car, but leaned in to her to make sure that her seat belt was secure. She looked up at him with wide eyes, but he quickly faced the windshield. "So where do you live?"

She told him the address, and he nodded,

driving in that direction. His mom's house was only two blocks away from hers, which meant he was familiar with the neighborhood. He turned the radio off, but jacked up the heat in case she was cold. "Feeling any better?"

She shook her head and groaned. "I'm never drinking wine again."

"I wouldn't go that far. You might want to have a decent meal before you do it again, though." He glanced at her. "I told you those spit buckets were there for a reason."

"It seemed so unsanitary." She closed her eyes again. "I should have, though. I didn't realize it would have such an effect on me. But then, I'm not much of a drinker. Lesson learned."

He chuckled. "You'll be feeling that lesson tomorrow I'm betting." He made a sharp right turn onto her street. "Do you have someone who could stay with you tonight? Maybe Page?"

"I'll be fine. I'm going straight to bed."

"I'd feel better if you had someone with you." He glanced out the window, trying to read the house numbers.

She pointed at a light blue cottage on the right. "It's that one there."

The house suited her, petite, dependable, painted in pastel colors, featuring big windows with lacy curtains. He pulled into the driveway, and she started to open the door. He held out his hand. "Let me help you inside."

"I'm not completely useless."

"Didn't say you were, but you're still unsteady on your feet. You don't want to slip on the ice and break your ankle." He got out and walked around the car to her open passenger door. He waited as she slowly emerged, then held tightly to him as he put his arms around her waist. They lumbered up the path, and he took her house keys from her when she fumbled with them. Once inside, she flicked on a nearby light switch and he took in the cozy atmosphere. She had lots of pillows and a multicolored crocheted blanket over the back of an overstuffed sofa. An antique rocking chair with another blanket that looked handmade was next to a jam-packed built-in bookcase. Candles on every surface. He walked her to the sofa and laid her down. "Where's your bathroom?"

She pointed. He found the bathroom as well as a washcloth from a stack on a floating shelf. He turned on the faucet and wet the washcloth, then returned to April and placed it on her forehead. "This will give you some relief."

She groaned. "I doubt it. Is it going to make me forget how I embarrassed myself back there?"

"Probably not for a while." He took his cell phone from his coat pocket. "Now, what is Page's phone number? I'll ask her to come over."

"No." She took her phone from her pants pocket. "She won't answer if she doesn't recognize the phone number. Call her on mine."

He scrolled through her contact list, spotted Page's name, then pressed the call icon next to her name. Page picked up on the first ring. "So how was your date? Better than Mateo?"

"Page, this is Zach Harrison. I'm here at April's house since she's not feeling well. She needs a friend to stay with her."

"Oh." She paused. "I'll be right there. You won't go until I get there?"

He agreed and, after ending the call, left

the phone on the coffee table next to the sofa. He took a seat in the rocking chair. "You sure know how to show a guy a good time."

April covered her eyes with the washcloth. "I'm really not like this."

"If you were, we'd still be at the shop tasting wines."

"Please don't say that word." She puffed her cheeks out and exhaled. "You're really good at taking care of people. That's something I didn't expect."

"I've had a lot of practice with my mom. She hasn't been well for many years."

April removed the washcloth to look at him. "What does she have?"

He shook his head. He didn't share details about his mother outside the family unless it was with one of the caregivers he hired. Part of it was to protect his mother. More of it was because he didn't know how to explain what it meant to watch her regress into a child-like state. He didn't like to talk of the pain or anger he felt about her. Instead, he swallowed those feelings down and kept up appearances. "She's just not well."

"I'm a doctor. I could help."

He doubted it. He'd sought out the advice of many over the years, but none could stop the progression of the disease that robbed his mother of her memories. "I'm taking care of her. We'll be fine."

April peered at him, but dropped the topic. "I want to make it up to you for throwing up on your shoes."

He stared at them and sighed. Definitely ruined. He brought his gaze back up to hers. "It's fine. They were never my favorites."

She bit her lip. "But I feel guilty about it. Are you sure there's nothing I can do to pay you back for them?"

A thought niggled at the back of his brain. "Actually, there might be a way that you can. I need a date for a wedding."

April's eyes widened, and she put the washcloth back on her forehead. "As you saw tonight, I'm not exactly great date material."

"How can you say that? Before you got sick, I was having a good time getting to know you." He sat on the edge of the rocker. "I'm throwing a wedding for a potential client Sunday evening. It would mean a lot to me if you would agree to accompany me."

"When I said pay you back, I figured I'd give you money."

"This is more fun." He rubbed his hands together, pretty happy with himself for thinking of this. "Please, April. I don't know anyone else to take at this late date."

"You did put it off till the end."

Mostly because the only woman he wanted to take with him was the one lying on the sofa in front of him. "It's one night, only a few hours."

She finally nodded. "Fine. What time will you be picking me up?"

He smiled and rose from the rocking chair at the knock on the front door. He opened it to find Page standing on the porch. She pushed past him and rushed to the sofa. "Are you okay? What happened?"

April moaned. "Too much wine."

Page turned and glared at Zach. "You thought you could take advantage of her by getting her drunk?"

April reached out and touched Page's arm. "It's not his fault. I should have spit at the wine tasting, but I couldn't. I drank too much as a result."

Page slung off her jacket and dropped it on the floor. "You always were a lightweight." She glanced at Zach. "Is there a reason you need to stay?"

"No, ma'am." The cavalry was here, so he walked over to April and placed a hand on her forehead. "I hope you feel better. I'll call you tomorrow with details about Sunday." He turned to Page. "Thank you for taking care of her."

She gave him a nod and accompanied him to the door. He tried not to take it personally when she slammed the door shut and locked it behind him.

HER TONGUE FELT as if it had swollen to twice its size and left her mouth feeling full of cotton balls. "Page, can you get me a glass of water?"

Page returned moments later with a glass of water from the tap. April sat up and took the glass with both hands. After several tentative sips, she then looked at Page, who was looking closely at her. "What?"

"How did you end up going on a date with Dr. Ross and return home with Zach Harrison? Did I miss something?"

"Dr. Ross stood me up. Zach was there on his own, so we started talking. Then I got sick." She winced. "All over his shoes."

Page smirked at this and took a seat on the other end of the sofa. "I would have paid money to see that."

"Believe me, it wasn't pretty." She took more sips of water.

"And what is on Sunday?"

"I'm his date for a wedding." At Page's raised eyebrows, she gave a shrug. "It's the least I could do to make up for what happened. And besides, I'll get to check off another item on my list."

"Going to a wedding is on your list?"

"No, but finding the perfect little black dress is." She grabbed her journal from the coffee table and opened it. Smiling, she ran a finger over the words. "Number seven, the perfect LBD."

"And you think you're going to find it by Sunday?" Page scoffed. "Let's wait and see how you feel tomorrow morning. You might not be up to shopping."

"Who wouldn't be in the mood for shopping?"

APRIL'S HEAD POUNDED in rhythm to her heart-beat as she sat up in bed the next morning. She placed a hand against her forehead and groaned. Page appeared in the doorway and handed her a cup of hot coffee. "I thought I heard Sleeping Beauty waking up."

Despite the drink's temperature, April had a slug of the strong black liquid. "What time is it?"

"Almost noon."

April shrieked and got out of bed. Big mistake. Her stomach rebelled, so she closed her eyes and took a few deep breaths. "That wine sure packs a punch."

Page pushed her toward the bathroom. "You'll feel better once you take a shower and get dressed. Then we can talk about going to the mall for your dress."

April groaned but allowed herself to be guided away. She finished the coffee, handed the empty mug to Page before shutting the door and starting the water in the shower.

Twenty minutes later, she emerged from the bathroom, clean and dressed in a white T-shirt and skinny jeans. She'd forgone blow-drying her hair since the sound of the machine made her eyeballs ache and her teeth set on edge. Instead, she grabbed one of the ball caps from her closet. When she'd lost her hair, she'd worn a lot of these and she'd amassed quite a collection. She chose a Detroit Red Wings hat and pulled the bill low on her head.

In the living room she found Page glued to a cooking show on the television. She gave April the once-over and nodded. "I guess you'll do."

"It's just the mall."

Page rose to her feet. "You look like a truck ran over you, then backed up and hit you again."

"That's exactly how I feel." April noticed the mussed-up pillow and quilt on the sofa. "Did you spend the night?"

"I didn't want to leave you in your condition. I went home earlier for a shower and change of clothes, but came right back." Page looked at her from head to toe and grimaced. "We don't have to do this today."

"I need the dress for tomorrow night, so yes, I do have to." April pulled on her coat and zipped it up. "But I can do this on my own if you'd rather go home."

"Are you kidding me? I don't remember ever seeing you in a dress. This may be my only chance." She clicked off the television and put her coat on and followed April outside. She held up her car keys. "I'm driving."

Thank goodness. Her eyes and head hurt too much to be able to concentrate on anything but the basic functions of walking and talking. She got in on the passenger side of Page's car and turned off the radio as the ignition started. "No offense, but I can't do music right now."

Page snickered and backed out of the driveway. April closed her eyes as her friend drove them out to the suburbs to a mall that had every kind of clothing store imaginable. If she couldn't find the perfect little black dress there, then it didn't exist.

They didn't find it, however, until the eighth store. April emerged from the dressing room and positioned herself in front of the three-way mirror. Page whistled. "Now, that's a dress."

And it was. The sheath was sleeveless and had lace on the top that cut straight across her clavicles, making her feel covered but still sexy. She took a few turns in front of the mirror. "Will this work?"

"It's better than anything else you've tried on." Page approached her and looked at the price tag. "It should be perfect at this price."

"And that doesn't even include the shoes." April turned a few more times, looking at herself from all angles. "I deserve this, don't I?"

"After everything you went through to survive? Absolutely." Page plopped down in one of the chairs next to the changing room. "Are you going to try on the other dress or is this it?"

"I think this is it." She put a hand to her belly. "I've never owned anything so beautiful."

She slipped back into her T-shirt and jeans, then paid for the dress, which the sales clerk put in a thick plastic garment bag. April signed the credit card slip and put the garment bag over her arm.

As they walked past the food court, April tugged on Page's arm. "Can we get something to eat?" she asked. "I'm starving."

Page trailed April as she checked out the

different food venues. Her tummy still felt iffy, but a pretzel couldn't hurt, right? She ordered two, along with bottles of water, and slapped Page's hand as she reached for her wallet. "This is to pay you back for taking care of me and driving me around today."

"I'm surprised you can afford this after getting that dress." But Page put her wallet back in her purse and found them an empty table. She wiped it down with a wet wipe from her purse, then took a seat. "These places are so unsanitary."

"That's part of the fun." April placed one hot pretzel in front of Page, then ripped off a section of hers and popped it in her mouth. She closed her eyes as she chewed the warm, salty dough. "This was always my favorite part of coming to the mall."

"Why did you really agree to go with Zach to this wedding? And don't say it was because you ruined his shoes."

April opened her eyes and gave a shrug. "I don't know. I mean, a big part of it is because I felt guilty about what I did. But another part of me wanted to get to know him more."

"Why?"

She leaned back at Page's incredulous tone. "Because I might have misjudged him. He was so sweet last night to take care of me. And he didn't yell when I got sick on him. But even before that happened, he seemed…" She shrugged and picked at her pretzel. "I don't know. Maybe I'm wrong about him. Maybe my first impression was the right one."

"Do you honestly believe that?"

She recalled meeting him in the emergency room with Antonio. He'd seemed scared for his client, so maybe his brusqueness could be attributed to that. "No. But I'd like to give him a chance to prove me wrong. Maybe that's what this is about."

They finished their snack and started to head toward the shoe stores. Page paused once and put her hand at the small of her back. April stopped and waited for her friend to catch up to her. "Are you okay?"

Page grimaced. "I must have slept funny."

That answer didn't ring true with April. "How long have you been having lower-back pains?"

Page shook her head. "Don't."

"I'm just asking a question. How long?"

Page glanced at the stores before answering April. "About two weeks. I already made an appointment with my doctor, so I don't need a lecture, okay?"

"You know we've got to be on top of our health."

"It could be nothing."

April put a hand on Page's shoulder. "And it might be something. You'll let me know what the doctor says?"

Page pushed April's hand away. "You know I will. But it's probably nothing."

ZACH HAD NO clue why she'd actually agreed to be his date for the wedding, but as he arrived at April's house on Sunday night, he was glad she had despite feeling as if he were on a ship being tossed by the sea. He shut off his car, took a deep breath, got out and walked up the short path to the front door. He knocked and waited for her to open it.

"Wow." She certainly looked a lot better than the last time he'd seen her. She wore a simple black dress, but with her hair pinned back by sparkly clips and makeup applied expertly, she was stunning.

She gave him a smile and stepped aside so that he could enter. She reached down and grabbed high-heel shoes that would add at least three inches to her tiny frame. She put them on, leaning on him for balance, and grabbed a dark silver wrap. He helped her put it around her shoulders, and the nearness of her made his head spin. She glanced over her shoulder at him, and he lost what he'd planned to say. Instead, he cleared his throat and pointed to the door. "Shall we go?"

She nodded and placed her hand on his elbow as they left the house.

On the drive to the banquet hall, he stole glimpses of her at the same time as he was trying to keep his eyes on the icy road. "You look fabulous."

She ducked her head. "You do, too."

He waited for her to say more, remembering that she tended to go on, but she stayed silent, her gaze on the buildings going by. At the next red light, he adjusted his tie, then reached over and touched her hand lying in her lap. She withdrew it quickly, and he regretted the gesture. Maybe he was making more out of this than he realized. Maybe she'd agreed to this only to make up for ruining his shoes, after all.

He put his hand back on the steering wheel. "Sorry."

"No, it's okay. You startled me."

He noticed the light had turned green, so he drove on. "I've never thrown a wedding before, so this will either be a triumph or a tragedy."

"How? You were married before."

"Marissa took care of all those details. All I had to do was show up on the day in my tuxedo." He flipped on the right-turn signal to take them into the banquet hall parking lot. "In all fairness, my assistant helped with a lot of the organizing for tonight. I may get the credit, but he certainly deserves some, too."

He parked and pressed the button to pop the trunk open before getting out of the car. "I have to take in some last-minute decorations and favors. Do you mind giving me a hand?"

April got out and joined him at the back of the car. She touched one of the centerpieces. "Daisies?"

"The bride's favorite." He hefted two of the floral arrangements in his hands. "Do you know how hard it is to find fresh daisies around here in the middle of winter? But Dalvin is a genius."

"Dalvin?"

"My assistant."

She gave a nod and grabbed two more centerpieces. In the banquet hall, they placed the decorations on the first table. April glanced around the spacious room and whistled. "Your assistant did all this?"

Zach arranged the centerpieces on the different tables. "Actually, my nonna helped us put this together after church." He propped his hands on his hips and gave a satisfied nod as he took in the fantastic job they'd done to transform a large, blank ballroom into an intimate setting. Dalvin had found a lattice archway under which Chris and his wife would get married. Zach had spent an hour weaving white Christmas lights in and around the archway to give it a soft glow. He had to admit that he liked the effect. "We did pretty good."

April moved another centerpiece into the middle of a table. "I'd say so. I'd like to get married here."

"So, you know I've been married before. You?" When she shook her head, he stopped and stared at her. "Why in the world haven't you? Are all your boyfriends blind and kooky?"

She smiled and took a centerpiece from him. "I've been married to my career for the last eight years. It hasn't come up."

"Not even close?"

"Nope." She set the floral arrangement in the perfect spot and turned to face him. "Were there more of those in the car?"

"A few."

She accompanied him to his car, thrust several arrangements into his arms, grabbed the last three for herself and slammed shut the trunk door.

"I don't get it," he said.

"What's that?" Back in the ballroom, she finished placing the flowers at the remaining empty tables before scanning the room.

"How has no guy snatched you up? You're smart. Pretty. You're a doctor, for Pete's sake." He walked up to her and put his hands on her shoulders. "You're the whole package."

She stepped away from him and wandered

over to the head table, where she straightened the engraved champagne flutes. "Can you drop the subject? I don't want to talk about that."

"Do you date?"

She held out her hands. "What did I just say?"

"We don't have to talk about marriage. I want to know why you're not dating."

"Why? Are you planning on changing that?"

He sighed and ran a hand through his hair. "I don't date either. Like you, my career takes up a lot of my time. And besides, my plate is already full."

"Then you'll understand that I have the same reasons."

"A woman like you should have someone."

"I have friends. And that's enough for me."

He took a few steps toward her and raised one eyebrow. "Is it? Or was reentering the dating world on that second-chance list of yours?"

She blushed and he knew he had her on that point. His cell phone buzzed, and he tapped out a response to Dalvin's question. "My assistant is here with the rest of the supplies. I need to go let him in."

When he'd taken a few steps, she called his name. He stopped and turned to face her. "A man like you should have someone, too."

He gave a nod at this, then left the reception hall to meet his assistant in the parking lot. Maybe he did, but there was no room in his life for anyone else.

THE WEDDING CEREMONY took less than twenty minutes, but April considered it one of the most touching and heartfelt she'd been blessed enough to witness. The way the bride and groom looked at each other as if they had the room alone to themselves. Or how the groom touched the bride's cheek before kissing her and making her his wife. She'd had to dab the corners of her eyes at that one.

And she'd looked away to find Zach watching her with a smirk. Okay, so she was a sentimental fool. She got teary at weddings and loved reading romance novels. Zach's earlier insistence that she needed someone had hit her hard. When she had turned thirty, she told herself she'd give herself five years to figure out balance in her life. She had let her career consume her, losing time with family and friends, even canceling holiday plans and dates. Her life in the hospital had been everything.

Then, almost two years ago, due to a cancer diagnosis, things had started to shift. If she couldn't find balance, her body would quit on her. She couldn't put in the long hours that she was used to as the side effects of chemo and radiation took their toll. But even now, as she stood with a champagne flute of sparkling grape juice in her hand, she could admit that she still hadn't found balance. That's why she'd needed the second-chance list. It was her reminder to live life, rather than work it.

She had some of the juice, then spotted Zach when he called her name. "You look deep in thought," he said.

"Weddings and funerals tend to do that to me." She noted the beautiful room again and all the happy guests. "You really pulled off a beautiful wedding."

"Thank you." The familiar buzzing sounded in his pocket. He pulled out his phone and frowned at the screen before shoving it back. He stared at the bride and groom, laughing as they swayed on the dance floor. "They're a great couple and they deserved a magical night."

"You certainly gave it to them."

She thought about asking him to join her on the dance floor when he got out his phone and walked away. Okay, so that was a little rude. What was it with him and his love affair with that phone?

At the lavish buffet, she found Mrs. Rossi surveying the choices and filling a plate. The older lady looked up and smiled at April. "Zach told me he was inviting you tonight. You're looking lovely."

April put a hand on her belly and shuffled from one foot to the other. She'd never been good at taking compliments, so she shrugged it off and took a plate from the stack. "Maybe. If anyone looks good tonight, it's you. Deep purple is your color."

Mrs. Rossi wrinkled her nose. "It's the color of old ladies. But since this was last-minute…" She gave a wave of her hand and then spooned pasta onto her plate, adding a giant scoop to April's. "You have to try this baked ziti. It's one of Silvio's specialties. I told Zach he had to include it on the menu."

"You know the chef?"

"Chef. Manager. Owner. Silvio does it all."

Mrs. Rossi continued down the buffet table, April following her and putting on her plate what the older woman recommended. They took a pair of seats at one of the emptier tables and tucked into their meals. Another slow song with violins started and April glanced at the dance floor, where more couples had joined the bride and groom. Mrs. Rossi dabbed at her mouth, putting the cloth napkin back on her lap. "You should go out there and join them."

"Dancing alone isn't much fun." April glanced around the room for Zach and saw him standing near the exit, phone glued to his ear. "Is he always like that?"

Mrs. Rossi turned and looked at her grandson. "Zach has a lot going on. Maybe too much. I'm sure whatever is pulling him away from you is important."

"We're not dating."

The older woman raised one eyebrow and

took a long sip of water. She winked and focused again on her meal. "If you say so."

"I know so. Zach needed an escort for this evening and I owed him a favor." She pushed a fork through the ziti. "That's all this is."

Mrs. Rossi didn't look as if she'd bought April's answer. She pointed at April's still-full plate. "Not hungry, dear?"

She took a bite of the ziti. It practically melted in her mouth. "Mmm. What does he put in this to make it so heavenly?"

"Come to my next class and maybe you'll find out. Have you been keeping up with the homework?"

"You mean making my own pasta?" April winced. "I'm afraid my job doesn't allow me much time to cook, as fun as it was."

"I could teach you some quick meals you can throw together in minutes." Mrs. Rossi reached for her handbag and pulled out a small, rectangular calendar. "When's your next day off? You can come to my house and we'll make a few things."

"Oh, I couldn't do that." It shocked her to think that this woman who had met her three times would invite her, a practical stranger, into her home.

Mrs. Rossi looked up at her, confusion in her eyes. "I wouldn't offer if I didn't want to do this. Now, when is your day off?"

"Thursday."

The older woman wrote it down and circled it. "Seven o'clock. Ask Zach for the address. Or better yet, a ride."

Just then, Zach appeared at the table and put a hand on the back of April's chair. He leaned down between the two women. "I have to go."

Mrs. Rossi nodded and started to gather her things. "I'll go with you."

"No. You know how she gets when she's really sick." He gestured to April. "Can you take her home, Nonna?"

"Who's sick? Maybe I can help. I'm a doctor." April dropped her fork on her plate and pulled the wrap over her shoulders.

"No, I'm going alone. Nonna can get you home. I'm sorry for running out like this, but it's an emergency."

April jumped to her feet. "If someone is ill,

it's my sworn duty to take care of her. And you will take me with you."

Mrs. Rossi shrugged. "She couldn't hurt, Zach. And maybe she can help."

"I don't need anyone's help, Nonna. And, April, I am not taking you anywhere." He backed away and strode across the room. He whispered in the groom's ear, then the two men shook hands and Zach left the banquet hall.

Mrs. Rossi thrust April's purse at her. "If you run, you can catch him. Despite what he says, he needs all the help he can get with his mother."

April nodded and ran toward the exit. She gave the heavy glass door a huge push and sprinted into the parking lot. Spotting Zach's sleek SUV, she darted in its direction and just managed to put her hands on the hood before he could put his foot on the gas. He beeped the horn, but she wouldn't move. He rolled down the window and stuck his head outside. "Move it, Sprader. I don't have time for this."

"Take me with you."

She could see the tight set of his jaw even in the dark, but knew she'd won when he waved her to the passenger door. She got in the car and put her seat belt on before looking at him. "What do I need to know?"

"You're staying in the kitchen and out of my way." He checked the mirrors and pulled out of the lot and onto the street. "I don't know what I'm going to be walking into. Just that it's a bad night."

"Bad night? Meaning what?" She put a hand on Zach's shoulder. "What are you talking about?"

"Just sit back and let me drive." He kept his gaze on the road ahead of them and didn't say a word until they got to a house a few blocks from her own. "Stay in the kitchen. Please."

He got out of the car and hustled up to the back door. April followed him inside and heard the shrieks right away. Zach disappeared down the hallway. A woman in scrubs sat at the dining room table, holding a bloody dish towel to her brow. April walked up to her. "Can I take a look?"

"Who are you?"

"Dr. Sprader. I work in the emergency room at the hospital." She removed the towel and dabbed at the wound that grazed just above the woman's eyebrow. "Looks superficial, so you won't need stitches. A bandage should be sufficient."

A loud scream from the other end of the house snapped April's head in that direction. "You'll be fine," she told the woman.

Then she ran down the hallway to stand at the open door and stare in at Zach, who held up his hands to his mom dressed in a bathrobe. She clutched a shard of a china plate in one hand as she hung on to the bedpost with the other. "Where is my husband? You've taken him away from me!"

"He'll be home soon. I promise."

"Always you promise." Her face crumpled and she lowered the broken piece of plate. "I miss him so much. I just want to see him."

Zach took a few steps toward her and removed the jagged piece of china from her hand. "Let's get you to bed." He removed the bathrobe and laid it on the recliner by the window.

"I'm so tired."

"I'll read you a story."

He helped his mom into the bed, then pulled

the covers to her chin. "What story do you want tonight?" he asked. *"Little Women?"*

She nodded, so he sat next to her and opened to a page near the beginning. Before starting to read, he glanced up and saw April standing in the doorway. "I heard her scream."

"She's okay now." He looked over at his mother. "Aren't you?"

"I'm so tired." There was no mistaking the exhaustion in the woman's voice.

He leaned in and kissed her forehead. "I know. Why don't you close your eyes while I read this chapter?"

April waited a moment as he read out loud, then she returned down the hallway to the bathroom where she found bandages and hydrogen peroxide. She took the items with her to the dining room. The night nurse, presumably, still held the towel to her head. April dabbed the wound with the peroxide and waited for the bubbles to stop fizzing before placing a bandage over the cut. "Is she like this most of the time?"

"I don't know. I just started a few days ago. But I'm not sure how much longer I'll last if it's going to be like this."

April took a seat across from her. "Alzheimer's?"

"That's what the son says." The nurse looked up at someone standing behind April. "I'm sorry I had to call you."

April peered over her shoulder and found Zach with his hands on his hips, his tie loosened and his shirt hanging out of his trousers. "You were right to call. This was bad." He glanced up at the nurse's bandaged brow and winced. "I'm sorry."

"Mr. Harrison, I don't know if…"

"She's not always like this."

The nurse stood and Zach took a step toward her. She held up a hand to him. "Please. I need to go home." She grabbed her coat and purse, and said, "I'll see you tomorrow at five."

He let out a sigh and nodded. Once the back door had clicked shut, Zach took a seat at the table and put his head in his hands.

"How long has your mom been like this?"

He kept his head down and gave a soft groan. "This aggressive behavior? About a month or so. It's been getting worse the last little while, though."

"I think we should take her in to the ER."

Zach shook his head. "No. She's sleeping now. It's fine."

"But it could be a sign that something else is going on. Zach, I'll go with you. They can check her out and get you some answers."

"I said no."

April took a seat next to him. "Who's her doctor?"

"Winsley. But he's not helping, as you can see."

"What about Dr. Gregory? He's really good. He's helped a lot of my patients and their families. I could give you his number."

Zach rose and went to stand at the window that overlooked the front yard. "I don't need any more numbers. I don't want any more doctors and their advice. I just want my mom back."

April had never felt so feeble, so inadequate. Emergency medicine was her specialty, and she knew only the basics when it came to Alzheimer's. Not nearly enough to help Zach.

"The doctors can help you manage the behavior, the progression of the disease. But they can't bring her back."

"I know." His voice cracked, and the sound of it splintered her heart. "But I wish they could."

They stayed silent for a moment, then he faced her, but didn't meet her eyes. "I need to stay here with my mom, so I'll call you an Uber."

CHAPTER SIX

ZACH CHECKED HIS mother's room to make sure she still slept, then walked into the living room and lay down on the sofa. He put an arm behind his head and stared at the ceiling. Still in his suit, he contemplated going to his room to change. Better to get the thing hung up before any more wrinkles set in. But just the thought of moving anywhere made him tired.

All of this made him tired. He couldn't keep doing this, but what choice did he have? Nonna had mentioned a nearby nursing home that specialized in cases like his mom's. That felt like he was giving up on her, and he wasn't ready to admit defeat. Better to keep her here where things were familiar to her. Though what was familiar and what was foreign were starting to blur in her mind. He could see that.

He heard the squeak of bedsprings and held his breath, straining to hear if it meant she'd rolled over or gotten out of bed. No footsteps down the hall. She'd just turned over in her sleep.

One night, he'd gone to his bedroom and fallen asleep without checking the doors to make sure they'd been locked. He'd woken up a few hours later to a loud knocking sound. He answered the front door to discover that a neighbor had found his mom wandering the neighborhood in her nightgown, searching for the cat that had died five years before. He'd made sure to double-check the doors every night since, as well as install an alarm.

Thinking of it, he groaned and got to his feet. The front door, check. He padded through the dining room and kitchen, down the few stairs to the back door. Check. He returned to the living room and armed the alarm. If she woke up and tried to get out, he'd know.

The worst part about the evening, besides having to leave the wedding early, had been the look on April's face when she'd seen him with his mom. He could handle disapproval or disappointment, but the pity written in the pinched eyebrows and straight line of her mouth left him hollow. He should have insisted she stay at the wedding. Never should have brought her here. And then for her to offer advice on what doctor his mom should see?

He yanked off his tie and shrugged out of his suit coat, dropping them over the back of a dining room chair. He unbuttoned the cuffs on his shirt and rolled up the sleeves. Rubbed a hand over his face, before returning to the sofa and lying back down. He couldn't deal with anything else. This day was over.

And it had had such a great start. Seeing April in that dress. Watching his newly signed client get married to the love of his life. And then enjoying the fruits of his labors. Well, his and Dalvin's labors. They'd really pulled it off.

More bedsprings. He paused his thoughts and waited for footsteps. This time, she did appear in the dining room and found him on the sofa. "Zach, have you seen the dog? I thought I heard him whining to get out."

"I already let him outside, Ma." He stood and walked toward her. Lucky had been gone longer than the cat. "I told you I'd take care of him."

She put a hand on his cheek. "You take such good care of all of us."

"Why don't we get you back to bed? You must be sleepy."

He started to put his arm around her shoulders when she slapped him. "Don't touch me! Don't you put your hands on me."

He took a few steps back from her. "I'm just trying to help you."

"I can go to bed myself. You don't have to keep putting your nose in my business." She crossed her arms over her chest and glared at him. "You're always telling me what to do."

"I'm sorry, Ma. Won't happen again."

Her frown softened and she gave him a nod. "Good."

He couldn't get a handle on her mercurial moods. Maybe April had been right. Maybe there was something else going on with her. He should call Dr. Winsley in the morning. See if they needed to readjust her medications or something. This behavior, the violence and the mood swings, couldn't continue. It would kill him if it did.

APRIL PUT HER purse on the coffee table and eagerly dropped down onto the couch. She removed the high-heel shoes that pinched her feet, which she rubbed before lying back and staring at the ceiling. What a night. Definitely not one she'd expected.

Her cell phone in the purse buzzed, and she sat up, pawing through it until she found the phone and put it up to her ear. "Hey, Page."

"I need details."

April checked the time on her cable box. "You at work?"

"I'm on break. Now, tell me how your date was. I need to live vicariously through you."

April chortled and got comfortable on the sofa. "There aren't many details to give you. He had to leave early to go home to take care of his mom."

"He lives with his mom?"

"That sounds bad, but it's true. She's got Alzheimer's, and he lives with her so he can look after her."

"Wow. That may change my mind about him."

"I know, right? It's like he's got this whole side of him that I didn't even realize existed.

And now that I know, it makes me like him even more." She sighed and rubbed the back of her neck. "His mom got violent with the night nurse, which is why we had to go to their place before the wedding was over. I watched him as he calmed her down, put her to bed and read her a story." She thought back on the scene. "It was like she was the child and he the parent. That's got to be tough on him. On top of what he already does for his clients and everybody else. I mean, when does he get to have time for himself?" Page remained silent. April glanced at her phone. "You still there? Or did I lose you?"

"You're falling for him."

"What? No, I'm not." She couldn't be. She barely knew him. She could admit that she wanted to get to know him better, but that was a far cry from being in love with him. "I just feel bad for him."

"I bet that went over well. Guys love when you pity them."

"I don't pity him."

"But you are interested in him."

April began to protest, then paused. She had to admit that he intrigued her and she longed to get to know him better. "Maybe I am. That doesn't mean I'm going to date him. The whole reason for my second-chance list is to find balance in my life. Less work, more fun. And if anyone has a more unbalanced life, it's Zach Harrison."

"So what are you going to do now?"

That was the big question. She could tamp down the feelings she had for him and pretend they were nothing. She could explore the feelings with him. Or she could ignore them and pray that they went away. She chose the latter. "Nothing. I'm going to keep working on my list. Next, I'm joining a gym."

Page harrumphed on the other end of the line. "You're not going to drag me with you, are you? I hate working out."

"You're a twig who doesn't need to. I'm fighting the belly bulge after going on those meds, so I need to do something. Yep. I'm going to the gym and forget all about Zach."

After talking for a few more minutes with Page, she quit the call and pulled up the search app on her phone. She typed in "new treatments for Alzheimer's" and started to scroll through the results, telling herself that wanting to help Zach's mother had nothing to do with him. It was practically her job to find out the latest information.

ZACH ENDED THE call with the scout for the Chicago club and checked the time. His grumbling stomach reminded him he'd skipped lunch again, and he pressed the intercom button to alert Dalvin. His assistant stepped into the office. "You rang?"

"Didn't we order lunch?"

"The rest of the office staff did three hours ago, but you never put in your request." Dalvin left the office and returned with a foam box and plastic utensils. "Lucky for you, I know what you like and I've been keeping it warm until you were ready to eat."

Zach lifted the lid and smiled. "Yes, you do know what I like."

As Zach ate his lunch, Dalvin settled himself in the chair across from him. "So you've got Ramos a tryout with Chicago?"

"Not yet, but they're interested." He wiped his mouth with a napkin and checked email on his computer. Frowned at an address that took him a moment to recognize.

ASprader@detroitgeneral.org. That woman would not give up. He opened the email and skimmed the message. She'd sent information on recent updates to Alzheimer's treatments. He didn't need her telling him what to do. He had enough doctors who thought they knew better than he did about what to do for his mother. He trashed the message.

On the other hand, if she knew something that they didn't… He changed his mind and retrieved the email from his deleted folder. "Can you do me a personal favor?"

"Another wedding?" Dalvin brightened.

His assistant looked too happy to be attempting that again. Zach shuddered at the thought. One had been enough for him. "More like research on developments for treating Alzheimer's disease." He reopened April's email. "And I need to call Dr. Winsley and get an appointment for my mother."

Dalvin wrote the information down on a sticky note and rose from the chair. "You got it." He checked the time on his step tracker. "And don't forget you have a conference call at four with the Lions about Johnson."

"Put them through when they call." He

turned back to his computer and opened the first of eight articles that April had sent him.

By the end of his day, he'd fielded an offer from the Lions for Antonio, had a doctor's appointment the following week for his mother and had read half of the articles. He settled himself in his car and headed toward home. He opened his car's hands-free phone system and had it call April. She didn't answer and the call went to voice mail. Checking his rearview mirror before making a lane change, he left her a message, keeping it simple and to the point. "Thank you for the advice. Call me."

APRIL'S PHONE BUZZED in her pocket again, but she ignored it as she tried to follow the trainer through the gym as he pointed out several machines. "These will work your abs as well as strengthening your core. You're not in bad shape, but the things I could do to your body would make your boyfriend weep."

She tried to ignore the sexual innuendo. "I don't have a boyfriend."

The trainer stopped and gave her a once-over. "Well, I can change that. Give me a month and men will be eating out of your toned hand." He stopped at a treadmill where a young guy ran at full tilt. The trainer pressed a few buttons so that the treadmill started to incline. "I don't take on anyone who tells me they can't. You can. And you will."

April took stock of the large room full of equipment. One of the emergency room nurses had recommended not only this place, but the trainer who'd gotten her into shape for the annual Detroit marathon last year. April knew she had to do something because exercise would improve her chances of survival and lower the risk of the cancer returning. "All right. I can."

The trainer smiled. "Good. We'll sign the paperwork in my office and discuss schedules and nutrition." He started toward the administration offices.

April accompanied him and tugged her phone out of her pocket. Zach had called and left a voice mail. She could barely hear his message over the blaring music in the gym. He'd gotten her email. Good.

After signing over her life and discussing meal plans, April left the gym. She started her car and waited for it to warm up before leaving. While she waited, she played with her phone. Should she call Zach now? Or hold off until she was home?

She pressed his name before she could second-guess herself. He picked up on the first ring. "April."

"Hi." She expected him to say something else, but he kept silent. "How's your mom doing today?"

"Better, I guess. No throwing dishes at least."

"Good."

Again, silence, during which she questioned why he'd asked her to phone him. She adjusted the heater so that the hot air blew on her faster. "So... Zach, you asked me to call?"

"Right. I got an appointment with Winsley for next week, but I was wondering if you had the name of that doctor you mentioned."

"Dr. Gregory. I can text you his information tomorrow when I'm at the hospital. Maybe he could find some of the answers you're searching for."

"Thank you."

She waited, but still he said nothing else.

"Do you have a problem with me?" She figured she'd ask the question that had been bothering her since the night before. "I mean, it's like you turned off all your charm. And I'm not sure what I did."

"It's not what you did." A pause. "Well, maybe it is. It's just I've been responsible for my mother for many years and I'm not good with accepting a hand from anyone else."

"You can't do this all on your own."

"Don't you think I know that?"

She blinked at the snap in his voice. "Well, good luck with her. And goodbye."

"April, wait. I don't mean to be short with you. I just… I don't know what to do anymore." His voice dropped softer. "And that scares me because I'm losing her more and more. Eventually, she'll be gone, and then what will I do?"

She took a deep breath. "Doctors like to believe they have all the answers, but the truth is we only know in part. We can tell you about the chemistry of the brain and how your mother's disease will progress, but we can't tell you how to cope. How to accept the inevitable. But I do know that you'll go on.

You'll live. Survive. Your life will look different than it is right now, but disease has a way of changing your priorities. You'll find what's important and hold on to that."

He gave a bitter chuckle. "That doesn't really help me."

"Because there is no help. But you can hopefully draw comfort from knowing you'll be okay in the end." She glanced out her window. "I'm speaking from experience. True, it was cancer that upended my world while you're experiencing this through your mom's Alzheimer's. But the end is the same."

"You sound like a shrink with all that talk."

"That's what helped me get through the worst year of my life. Affirmations that I was stronger than the disease. Belief that I'd come out better on the other side. Not just physically, but emotionally and spiritually. And I know you will, too."

There was silence on the other end as she waited for him to go on. His voice was raw, almost inaudible when he did. "All I wanted was to thank you for sending me all that information. I don't need you to tell me how to feel about what's happening to her."

"That's the thing. It's not only her that it's happening to. You're just as involved."

"I gotta go," he said and hung up the phone.

April sat in her car and stared. Maybe she shouldn't have lectured, but she didn't like hearing him sound so defeated. If she could help him, she would. And if she lost him in the process, she'd accept that, too.

ZACH KNOCKED AT his grandparents' place and waited until Pops answered and ushered him inside. "Don't blame me, son. It was your Nonna's idea."

Zach frowned at this. "What did she do?" A woman's laugh that didn't belong to his grandmother floated in the air. "April?"

Smirking, he followed the sound of her infectious laughter to the kitchen, where Nonna was showing April how to dredge chicken cutlets in egg, before coating them with Italian bread crumbs. He appreciated the way April intently watched the process and clapped when the finished product was placed into a skillet with olive oil. She probably gave everything that same kind of attention, and part of him wished she would turn her attention to someone other than him. His better half reveled in how she reached out to him, though, and tried to enter his life whether he wanted her to or not.

She turned and looked at him. "I didn't know you were coming to dinner."

"I didn't know you were learning to cook tonight." He approached Nonna and gave her a loud kiss on her cheek. "But I'm betting my grandmother knew we'd both be here."

Nonna reached up and patted his cheek. "Hoped you would, dear. I wasn't positive it would all come together like this." She used a fork to turn the cutlets in the skillet. "You want them to brown on both sides, but not burn."

April nodded and leaned over the skillet to peer at the chicken. "How do you know when it's done?"

Nonna brought out a meat thermometer. "Some cooks pierce the meat to see if the juices run clear. I prefer to rely on science."

Zach left the two women in the kitchen and joined Pops in the dining room, where he set the table for four. He handed a plate to Zach and pointed to the end of the table. "Your nonna has romance on her mind."

"She should know better." He placed napkins beside the plates as his grandfather laid out the silverware. "I'm not interested in romance."

"There's nothing wrong with coming home to the right woman."

"I thought that was Marissa at one time. And we both know how that turned out."

"Your ex-wife only wanted one woman in your life." He handed two wineglasses to Zach. "She couldn't handle that your mother would always come first."

He arranged the glasses on the table. "And why does Nonna think April would be any different?"

"She's a doctor, so she knows what it means to sacrifice her time for others' well-being. She understands the role of caretakers. And she wouldn't run when things got tough." Pops put his hands on his hips and surveyed the table, giving it a satisfied nod.

Zach peered at his grandfather. "Nonna thinks? Or you do?"

Pops waved his hands. "After fifty-three

years of marriage, it's the same thing, no? Let's go choose a wine from the cellar."

When April placed the platter of chicken parmigiana in the middle of the table, everyone chose to ignore the dark brown edges and instead oohed and aahed at the presentation. His grandparents sat at the head and foot of the table while Zach sat directly across from April. Pops lifted his glass, and everyone followed suit. "To my family and new friend who have gathered here to enjoy this wonderful meal tonight, I thank you and ask for blessings on you."

April smiled and swallowed a mouthful of her wine. She looked at him over the top of her glass before setting it down on the table. "Sorry the chicken is so brown. I got distracted by Mrs. Rossi making the sauce."

Zach tucked his napkin on his lap and said, "If it tastes half as good as it smells, I'm sure we'll enjoy it all the more."

They passed dishes around the table. Pasta. Chicken. Salad. Bread. All the elements of a good meal at his grandparents' home. His phone buzzed in his pocket, but he chose to ignore it. Instead, he focused on Nonna sharing a story about an eccentric customer at the store earlier that day. But the phone buzzed again. He put his fork down on his plate and checked the cell's display.

Night nurse didn't show up. And she's asking for you.

He looked up to find them all watching him. He gave a shrug. "I have to go." He put a hand to his chest. "I'm sorry, Nonna. I wish I could stay."

"The one you should apologize to is April, since she cooked dinner."

He glanced at her and offered a lopsided smile. "What I ate was wonderful. Thank you."

He left the dining room and walked to the foyer, where he started to put on his coat. Nonna appeared behind him with a plastic container. "Here. I made this ahead of time, just in case."

He leaned in and kissed her cheek. "She needs me."

"Or do you need her?" She handed him a glove that had fallen on the floor. "Someday you'll find that it was the same thing."

"I'm all she's got."

"She has us, too, but you won't let us help you."

"You remember the last time. She had a total meltdown and went after Pops with a spoon." He shook his head. "I'm trying my best to keep her calm."

"And how's that going?"

He grimaced and put on his gloves, took the plastic container and hugged his grandmother. "Thank you for the invite, but you can stop with the matchmaking."

"I'm your grandmother. That will never stop."

He smiled and left the house. He'd wanted one night to enjoy dinner and spend time with his family. And he couldn't even have that.

He kept his focus driving on the icy roads and wondered what he'd be walking into when he got home.

APRIL DRIED THE last dish and handed it to Mrs. Rossi, who placed it in the cupboard to the right of the sink. "Thank you for the cooking lesson tonight. I'm learning a lot from you."

Mrs. Rossi closed the cupboard door. "I'm sorry things didn't go quite as planned."

"You mean inviting your grandson to spend time with me in the hopes that there will be a spark between us?" Trying to sound nonchalant about it, she said, "He's got a lot going on."

"More than he needs to. I don't know if you noticed, but he has a hard time accepting help." She took the damp dish towel from April and draped it over the edge of the sink to dry. "I had another reason for offering you a cooking lesson. I need to do something about Zach."

April frowned. "I don't understand. What could I do?"

"You are another choice, another path. A chance at finding something more than taking care of his mother and his clients." She rested against the kitchen counter. "I love him, so please don't misunderstand me. I'm afraid of the day when his mother is no longer there."

"When did she first start showing symptoms?"

"Kate is my daughter, but Zach is very good at protecting her. For all I know, she always showed them. But he was about sixteen when I first learned of it. Christmas Eve, and she seemed okay. We had dinner, opened gifts and went to Mass. On the way home from church, she started talking about stopping by the police station to see Robert. The thing is, Bobby had died five years before."

"She thought he wasn't with the family because he was working?"

Mrs. Rossi nodded and wrung her hands together. "We dropped them off at home and figured it was just the stress of the holidays."

"But it got worse."

"Zach finally admitted to us that she'd been having erratic behavior for years." She rubbed the back of her neck. "I should have seen it. I should have known. But that boy had it solely on his shoulders for all that time."

"You can't blame yourself. He hid it from you."

"He was afraid we'd take her away and put her in a hospital."

She should have known that was why he was so reluctant to take his mom to the emergency room. He didn't want to lose her to the doctors or the disease. The problem was that he couldn't have both. The way the disease progressed would take her away eventually.

April squeezed the older woman's hand. "Thank you for sharing this with me. Zach is lucky to have you."

Mrs. Rossi patted her cheek. "I could say the same about you."

April left their house with a container of leftovers that she planned on enjoying during her break the next day at work. She put the container on the passenger seat and drove home, thinking about what she and Mrs. Rossi had discussed. When she got home, she put the leftovers in the fridge, brought her laptop in the living room and sat on the sofa while she searched for Alzheimer's treatments that could be done at home. She knew Zach had nurses round the clock, but there might be something else he could do.

Her cell phone buzzed, and she tore her eyes from the computer to glance at the other screen. A text from Zach. Sorry for leaving early. This is my life.

She swiped the home button and entered her code. Pressed the message program and reread the text. How is she?

She watched a few bubbles form on the next line and waited for his response. Fine.

She doubted that, but she wasn't going to call him out on it. Instead, she put her cell phone on the coffee table a few feet in front of her and tried to ignore its existence. She went back to the computer, but caught herself glancing at the phone. She shook her head and concentrated on the article about home care options. Well, tried to concentrate. After rereading the same sentence four times, she picked up her cell phone. How are you?

Fine, too.

Somehow I don't believe that.

She waited a moment for him to respond, but gave up and put the phone next to her on the sofa. She exited out of the article she'd been reading and typed in the search engine: "taking care of the caregiver." Most of the results were geared toward those already caring for a family member. She did find an article written by a husband of a woman who was helping her aged mother. He described little things he did to help his wife as she poured all her energies into looking after someone else. She snatched a notepad and pen from a basket at the foot of the sofa and wrote down some ideas. She could do this for Zach.

Her phone buzzed. You don't know what it's like.

He was right about that. She didn't know. But she remembered what it was like to fight her own disease. So explain it to me.

How much time do you have?

She smiled and swiped her finger over the words of his text. All night if you need it.

Her phone stayed silent, and she returned to her computer. She clicked on another article about self-care suggestions for caregivers when her phone started ringing. She smiled as she answered it. "Hi, Zach."

"Why do you care?"

"Because you seem like a good man."

He chuckled. "That's not what you thought when we first met."

"Maybe I've changed my mind since then."

She settled into the pillows on the sofa as

he described what he'd been doing to take care of his mom. She didn't offer suggestions or solutions. She simply sat back and let him talk. And he had a lot to say. She guessed that he'd been holding on to most of these thoughts, afraid to share. But now that the dam had broken, they poured out of him, swirling waters of emotions flowing with the words. She had to grab a tissue once to stem her own emotions but kept listening.

After forty minutes, he sighed on the other end. "Sorry."

"For what?"

"I didn't realize all of that was in there."

She smiled. "Then I'm glad I was around to hear it."

CHAPTER SEVEN

ZACH RUBBED HIS eyes and tipped back in his office chair. Glancing at the clock on his computer, he noted it was just past eleven and he'd finally finished his last phone call of the morning. Well, second-to-last phone call. He dialed Chris's number and waited while it rang. The voice mail message started, then immediately stopped. "Just a minute, man. I'm right here."

He knew phoning his new client during his honeymoon probably wouldn't make him agent of the year, but his reason for the call just might. Patiently, he waited until Chris came back on the line. "You've got news, don't you?"

Zach smiled, even though the kid couldn't see him. "Chicago has come back with a counteroffer to what we presented. But I think you'll be pleased."

"How many millions pleased?"

"Four point two for two years with a five million bonus if you sign for a third." Zach smiled. "I told you that you'd like it."

"This is the best wedding present you could have given us."

"Then I can take back the bread maker I gave you?" Zach shifted and looked out his window at the cloudy skies. "Enjoy your honeymoon. We'll hammer out the finer details when you return in a couple days."

"Thanks again, man. You delivered everything you promised."

Zach hung up the phone, pleased with himself. He was known for making things happen for his clients. He used to believe the same about helping his mom. She needed him, and he was happy to be there for her. To take her to doctor appointments. To live with her so he could watch over her. But lately, the responsibility had started to chafe like a too-tight collar around his neck. Part of it was because her care required more than he could give. He no longer knew how to provide what she needed. When he was a little boy, she needed his smiles and hugs. As he got older and the disease started to take hold of her mind, she needed someone to take responsibility. And he'd gladly shouldered that. He was her only child so he had felt privileged to be able to do this for her. Lately, it had felt more like an obligation.

He rested a hand on his cell phone. Talking to April the night before had helped unload some of the weight from his shoulders. She'd reassured him that he wasn't a bad son because he'd begun to resent his mom. Said it was a normal part of being a caregiver to a loved one.

She'd also recommended a support group, but he'd quickly put a kibosh on that. There was no way in the world he was going to sit in a group of strangers and tell them about his mom. He'd kept his mom's illness a secret for so many years that sharing it felt like he was betraying her. He'd promised over the years to not tell anyone when she forgot appointments or how to drive home. She'd made him swear to keep what she called her slipups just between them. Until it had become necessary to tell his nonna because he was sixteen and afraid of his mom's erratic behavior.

He put his cell phone in his pocket and

stood, grabbing his suit jacket from the back of his desk chair. He walked out of his office and stopped at Dalvin's desk. "I'm going to lunch."

Dalvin squinted at the time on his computer. "It's almost noon. Congratulations for eating lunch at a normal time today."

"Let me know when the contract from Chicago arrives, and set up a meeting with Antonio for next week. Lunch or dinner at that restaurant he likes in Ferndale." He shrugged into his wool winter coat. "Do you want me to pick you up something while I'm out?"

"Only if it's gluten- and dairy-free." Dalvin wrinkled his nose. "New diet."

Zach gave a nod. "I'll try." He left the office and took the elevator down to the parking garage. He slipped into his car and tried to muster enthusiasm for eating lunch alone. Most of his meals were eaten with clients or coaches. Otherwise, he ate at his desk while he answered emails or held conference calls. The thought of eating in his office left him feeling…alone.

He should feel flush with success. He'd signed two clients in the past week with big futures in their respective sports. One a tennis pro, the other a graduating college senior who looked to go near the top in the upcoming football draft. He was on top of the world, right? So why did those victories feel empty?

He pulled out of the parking garage and headed to the hospital. Maybe he could treat April to lunch to show his appreciation of her having listened to him. Whom was he kidding? He wanted to see her, plain and simple. It wasn't the idea of eating alone that made him jumpy. It was the desire to catch a glimpse of her, if only for five minutes.

Parking spots near the front of Detroit General were scarce, so he parked the car at the back and briskly walked to the doors of the emergency room. He stopped at the admissions desk and asked for April. The nurse looked him up and down, sporting a huge grin on her face. "So you're the one."

He frowned at this. "Sorry?"

"She's had a spring in her step today. I assume you're the reason." She pressed a button on the phone on the desk, then picked up the receiver. "I'll tell her you're here. You can wait with the rest of them until she's free."

He removed his coat and took a seat in the waiting room, questioning his decision. Hacking coughs, cuts and wounds, and what looked like a woman ready to give birth surrounded him. He watched as patients were taken one by one to the treatment area. He tapped his fingers on the armrests of the plastic molded chair he sat in. Glancing at his watch and noting the time, he stood and shrugged back into his coat.

"Zach? Is everything okay?"

He turned and smiled at April. "I'd hoped to take you to lunch, but I should have realized you'd be busy."

"One of the other doctors called in with a personal problem, so we're short staffed. I'll be lucky to grab a sandwich from the cafeteria later." She patted his arm. "But thank you for thinking of me. That's really sweet of you."

Zach blinked. Sweet? Was she already putting him in the friend zone? Not that his life allowed room for much more than friendship at the moment. "Maybe another time."

"I'd like that." She glanced behind her and held up a finger to one of the nurses who had called her name. "They need me. I'll talk to you soon."

He nodded, watching as she sprinted down the hall toward the treatment area. Well, he'd wanted five minutes of her time, and he'd gotten almost that. He walked out to the parking lot and sat in his car. Still hungry, he debated his options. There was the diner across the street. As good as any, he figured and left his car to cross the avenue.

APRIL SNAPPED OFF the plastic gloves and threw them in a designated receptacle before leaving the empty trauma room. She shuddered at the bloody mess of gunshot wounds, something she'd gotten used to over the years. She'd left the northern Michigan tourist area she'd grown up in to come to the Detroit area because she'd wanted to help where it was needed most. And the need here overwhelmed her most days.

She noticed a group of nurses and doctors gathered around the reception area where Janet usually directed traffic and answered calls. "I'm telling you, he dropped it off and told us to enjoy it."

April tapped one of the doctors on the shoulder. "What's going on?"

"Some guy bought lunch for all of us from Doc's Diner across the street." He held a bagel sandwich in one hand. "And he said to thank you for it."

April looked over at Janet, who confirmed it. "Your boyfriend is very generous. There's enough food here for everyone on staff today."

Zach did this? They couldn't have lunch together, so he'd brought food for the entire staff? There were boxes and boxes of sandwiches and salads. Everyone was looking at her. "He's a friend."

"Nice friend." The doctor with the bagel took a bite of his sandwich and walked off.

The staff started to claim boxes and disappear where they could to get a quick bite before their next deluge of patients. April took a seat on the corner of Janet's desk. "I was not expecting this."

"I told him he didn't have to do it, but he insisted." Janet sorted through the boxes and took one that held what looked like a salad. "If you don't want him, will you give me dibs?"

April peered at the white-haired nurse who was not only married, but a mother and grandmother. "You got it."

She randomly picked a container and opened it. Greek salad with grilled chicken, her favorite. She'd just gotten a plastic baggie that contained silverware and a napkin when the emergency room doors crashed open. Janet took the salad from April. "I'll put this in the lounge for you."

She appreciated that. Lunch could wait because her patient being brought in on a gurney wouldn't.

Three hours later, April collapsed on the sofa in the staff lounge and closed her eyes. Her night-shift replacement would arrive shortly. She got up and walked to the fridge to find her salad. Janet had written her name in marker and an admonition to keep hands off. She smiled and grabbed it along with a bottle of water. She returned to the sofa and started to eat. Halfway through her meal, she grabbed her cell phone from her pocket and sent off a quick thanks to Zach.

His response came instantly. U R welcome.

You didn't have to do that.

Yes I did. U needed to eat. No big deal.

April took another bite and smiled as she chewed. She could get used to being spoiled like this.

But they were just friends. No reason to expect more.

APRIL SIGHED AND wound the yarn around her fingers as Perla had showed her. "What am I doing to mess this up? I'm not getting the hang of it."

Her friend Sherri's mother, Perla, took the knitting needles and yarn from her and pulled out several stitches. "Knitting is supposed to relax you, not tie you up in knots."

"Well, knots are all I seem to know how to do."

April watched as Perla started the row over for her and handed it back to her. "You're thinking too far ahead. Concentrate on the stitch you're on. Not the next one."

She accepted the needles, then looped the yarn around them. She moved the knitting needle over, then under the yarn before completing the loop. It should be easy. Definitely looked that way when she had first seen Perla demonstrate it. But now, she noted the mess left on the needle and sighed again. "Whatever made me think that knitting was something to put on my second-chance list?"

"Sherri mentioned that you were working your way through a list." Using curved needles, she returned to her own project, which looked like socks. "How is that going?"

April held up the needles. "About like this. It seemed simple enough when I first started writing what I wanted to do, but now, I'm having my doubts."

"What's next on your list?"

"I'm planning a trip to New York to see a Broadway musical, but it might have to be delayed until I have more time to do what I want to do. " She did another stitch, then exclaimed when the yarn did what it was supposed to. "I did it!"

"Because you're thinking less."

"Story of my life. Think and not do." She attempted another stitch and chastised herself as she had to remove it. "Some things on the list will have to wait for better weather or having time off. Some need money. But I'll get them all done. Just you wait."

"Sherri's mentioned making her own list." Perla stopped knitting and stared off into space. "For when she's better."

April reached over and touched the older woman's hands. "She'll get there. She's almost finished with radiation, and then they'll confirm the cancer is gone. And it is. I know it in my gut."

"I hope you're right."

April gave a small nod and returned to her row of uneven stitches. She wrinkled her nose and pulled out a few before attempting to make more. "I really appreciate you offering to teach me this."

"When Sherri mentioned it, I jumped at the chance. I'd hoped that she would want to learn, too, but she hates sitting around. Always on the go, that one." Perla's needles flashed as she knitted. "Trying to keep up with her brothers, I suspect."

"I miss my brother. He's still up north in the UP." She paused with the yarn and set it down in her lap. "It's hard not having family in the area."

Perla gasped and put her hand to her mouth. "Well, why didn't you say so? You're more than welcome to join us for the holidays if you're around."

"Thanks. I work most holidays so my colleagues with families can have the time off." She picked up her knitting again. "And I hang out with friends sometimes."

"I'll make sure Sherri invites you to the next family dinner."

"That would be nice. I've always thought that family is what you make it. You don't have to be born into a family to belong to it." She bit her lip as she tried a few more stitches, then surrendered and handed the chaos to Perla. "Can you show me one more time?"

ZACH NOTICED THE strange car parked in front of the house, but dismissed it since vehicles usually lined both sides of the street. Didn't mean anyone was there. He pressed the key fob to lock his car doors and picked his way carefully through the ice and snow to the rear of the house. Opening the door, he could hear talking right away. Inside, he followed the voices to the dining room, where he found April speaking to Dolores. They had their heads bent over some papers on the table. The nurse looked up at him and started to gather what they'd been huddling about. "Sorry, I didn't know when you'd be coming home."

Zach raised a brow at April, whose cheeks had become a deep pink. "Did you say you were coming by?" he asked, positive of her answer.

She shook her head. "I found something that I thought might be of interest with respect to taking care of your mother, so I stopped here on my drive home from work." She took the papers from Dolores and handed them to him. "It's about alternative therapies for those with memory issues. Herbal remedies and supplements that seem to aid in cognitive development and retention."

Zach looked briefly at the top article before tossing the papers back on the table. "And you think I haven't tried some of these?"

"You probably have, but knowledge is power." She pointed to one of the supplements.

"I've treated several patients who have found success with this one."

Zach removed his scarf and coat, and dumped them on the nearest empty chair. When he looked at both women again, it seemed as if they were expecting him to yell at them. Instead, he sighed and nodded. "I'll read them, I promise, but I've kept on top of the research out there. If it's been written, I've seen it."

April said, "I wanted to repay you for treating us all to lunch the other day. I figured this was one thing I could do."

"It's not that I don't appreciate it, but I didn't buy you lunch so you would do something for me."

April raised her chin. "I just wanted to do something nice for you."

She put on her coat, and Zach reached over to help her when she struggled to find a sleeve. She turned abruptly, and they nearly bumped heads. Instead, he found himself staring into her baby blue eyes. "Thank you for thinking of me. Of us."

She swallowed, and he saw the muscles in her neck contract and release. He considered reaching up and touching that muscle, but realized that Dolores was watching them. "I'm going to check on my mother."

"She had *Judge Judy* on. You know how she loves that show." Dolores glanced at the clock on the wall. "Do you want me to wait for the night nurse?"

Zach waved at her. "I'll be home until she gets here. See you in the morning."

Dolores's gaze flicked between him and April, and she covered a smile with her hand as she left the room to retrieve her things. She made her goodbyes and left through the back door. April sighed. "I should get going, too. I have some knitting to do."

Zach squelched a smile. "Another item on your list?"

"I thought it might be relaxing. In fact, it's the opposite, it's driving me crazy." She pounded her fist into her palm. "But I will figure it out. Even if it kills me."

"You could stay for dinner." Zach paused. Had he really said that aloud? He'd been thinking it, and it had flown out of his mouth on its own accord. "I don't have anything that's fancy, but I'm sure we can figure something out." He started to search through the cupboards and brought out two cans of soup. "Chicken and dumplings? Or split pea?"

April shook her head and put her purse strap over her shoulder. "As tempting as they may be, I need to get home. I have a big day tomorrow, and I want to be in bed early tonight."

"Busy at work?"

"More like having some tests done. Want to make sure the cancer is staying away." She wrapped her pink scarf around her neck. "Another reason I need to relax. These doctor visits still make me nervous. I'll probably toss and turn all night."

"You think the cancer has returned?"

"It's been almost a year cancer-free, and I still worry about the what-ifs. I know the statistics are in my favor, but my friend Page wasn't so lucky."

"She's still with us, isn't she?"

April smiled and took a deep breath. "Have a good night. You and your mom."

"Please stay. I'll distract you and keep your mind off tomorrow's appointment." He shook the cans of soup. "And I'll feed you."

"Zachary, are you home?" his mom yelled from her bedroom. "I'm hungry. Is it dinner yet?"

He glanced down the hall toward his mom's room and sighed. "Duty calls."

She unwound the scarf from her neck and placed it and her coat over the counter, then she took the cans of soup from his hands. "I'll heat dinner while you check on her."

"Are you sure you don't mind helping?" The idea of them working together to care for his mom warmed his insides.

April shooed him away as she began to open cupboards, needing to find a pot. Zach pointed to the cupboard above the stove. "They're in there. I'll be right back."

He left April to it and walked down the hallway to his mother's bedroom. When he opened the door, she sat up in her recliner and clapped her hands. "You are home. How was work?"

She seemed lucid, which he took as a good sign. "It's been really busy getting Tom ready for the draft in a few weeks. How was your day?"

"That woman kept bossing me around."

She pouted, but it softened to a smile when he kissed her on the cheek. She reached up and put a hand on his head, ruffling his hair. "You keep growing on me. Soon you'll be married and leaving me."

"I'm not getting married anytime soon, Ma." And it wasn't like he could leave her. "My friend April is making some soup for dinner, and if you're good you can have an ice-cream bar after."

"They're my favorite."

"I know." He felt like a father rewarding his young daughter, but then he'd slipped into that role years ago. "Do you want to eat dinner in your room or would you like to go to the dining room?"

"Where are you eating?"

"Wherever you are."

They ended up eating off trays in his mother's bedroom. April had placed a small plate with crackers next to the bowls of soup. His mother could feed herself, but it was much like a toddler learning how to use a spoon. April didn't wince or make faces as the soup dribbled down his mother's chin. Instead, she reached up with a napkin to wipe it away.

His mother peered at April. "Who is your friend, Zach?"

"April. She's a doctor."

His mother's eyes got wide, and she started to shake her head. "I don't like doctors. They hurt me."

Zach put his spoon down and rubbed his mother's shoulder. "April won't hurt you. She's my friend."

"I promise I won't hurt you, Mrs. Harrison."

His mother looked between them. "Promise?"

April nodded and held up her hand to swear to it. "I'm just Zach's friend who came over for dinner."

"Okay." His mother pushed the bowl of soup away. "I'm done. Can we have ice cream now?"

She'd eaten more than half of the soup, which Zach counted as a victory. Feeding her could be difficult at times, and he attributed her easiness to having company. He agreed and left the bedroom. In the kitchen, he retrieved three paper-covered ice-cream bars from the freezer. When he returned, he found

April brushing his mother's hair. She looked up at him and shrugged. "She mentioned that she wanted to fix herself up a little."

"April's good at hair," his mother informed him. "She's gentle with her hands. Maybe you should be a hairdresser instead of a doctor, dear. You'd be great."

April chuckled and continued pulling the brush slowly through his mom's hair. "Maybe if this doctor thing doesn't work out, it would be a nice fallback." Her gaze held his, and she winked.

That wink sent his heart soaring. To see her there interacting with and caring for his mother with such ease made it feel like he could have a normal life. That the burden he carried could be one he shared.

After her hair had been brushed, his mom let April help her get into her pajamas. Zach read a chapter from *Little Women* until his mother fell asleep, then he and April tiptoed out of the room. Zach closed the door and leaned against it. "Thanks for doing that."

April nodded. They carried the dirty dishes from their dinner to the kitchen and placed them in the sink. April started the water. Zach leaned over and turned off the faucet. "I'll do that later. Do you want to sit down in the living room?"

April stifled a yawn. "I really do have to get home. Lucky thing I don't live far from here." She walked into the dining room and retrieved her coat and purse. "Your mom had a good night."

"She was due for a few. It's been difficult lately. Her moods are all over the place. And the violent streak has been increasing." He leaned on the back of a chair and clasped his hands in front of him. "I was starting to worry that I might have to put her in a facility."

The crease between April's eyebrows furrowed deeper. "Just because she was docile tonight doesn't mean that she won't be violent tomorrow. That's not how this disease works. It gets worse, not better."

That's what he'd been worried about. He'd hoped that the calm he'd experienced with her would continue. He'd been navigating on eggshells long enough, hoping that he wouldn't spark an outburst from her. He couldn't be expected to live the rest of his life that way. Could he?

She hugged him gently. "If you need anything…"

He closed his eyes, put a hand under her chin and kissed her softly. He rested his forehead against hers. "You've done enough. Thank you."

She bit her lip and nodded before leaving.

THE CROWD AT the Hope Center was a little light for a regular meeting. Sherri had showed, but she looked tired as she slowly lowered her body into one of the metal folding chairs. Page wouldn't be there since she had to work, and a few others hadn't yet appeared. April took a seat next to Sherri and offered her one of the bottles of water she'd brought over from the refreshment table. Sherri thanked her and twisted off the cap before taking a sip. "I've been so thirsty lately."

"It's the radiation. Dehydrates you, so make sure you push the fluids." April opened her own bottle of water, but didn't take a drink. "How are you feeling otherwise?"

"Okay, I guess. More tired than normal."

She adjusted the scarf on her head. "Only one more week of this, then I'm done."

"Then your body can rest." April gave Sherri's hand a squeeze. "You're almost there, kiddo. I know you're going to be fine."

"I'll be fine once the doctor tells me that the cancer is officially gone."

"I remember that day. In fact, we're coming up on my one-year anniversary, and I plan on throwing a party to celebrate. You and Agent Hottie will come, right?"

Sherri smiled. "You've been there for me, so you bet I'll be there for you, cheering you on." She sipped her water and pointed at the circle of vacant chairs. "Where is everyone tonight?"

"If they're lucky, on a beach down south somewhere. Or in Page's case, doing her shift at the hospital. I'll be glad when her night rotation is over. I don't get to hang out with her as much when we're on opposite shifts."

More women filed in and Lynn, the group's leader, entered the center of the circle. "Before we get started, I want to remind everyone that we're having a fundraising dinner next month. Tickets can be purchased anytime. Since I don't see any new faces, who would like to kick off our sharing time tonight?"

April's eyebrows rose as Sherri raised her hand. Usually, Sherri listened as others talked about their lives, gave encouragement, clapped at the end. But sharing a story? This was a first.

Lynn smiled at Sherri and took a seat. Sherri sat up a little taller in her chair. "I have one more week of radiation, and then my treatment will be behind me. Which has gotten me thinking about what comes next. What happens after treatment? I mean, April's got her second-chance list to work on. But what am I going to do?"

"What do you want to do?" Lynn asked.

Sherri looked hesitant and was silent at first. "I want to enjoy my life with my husband and our adopted son. Shouldn't that be enough?"

April put a hand on her arm. "Is that enough for you?"

"The thing is, before cancer, I was single and alone. Now I have this family, so I don't know what a life is with them without cancer. A life that doesn't include treatments that make me sick and tired." Sherri chuckled. "Marcus might like to finally have a mom who isn't cranky or nauseous all the time or who keeps asking him to be quiet so she can rest. He might like to have a mom who can be as active as he is."

Lynn smiled. "So you want to become more active."

"I want to get to know this new body. I want to find my limits and what I'm capable of doing." Sherri looked at the circle of faces. "I want to find a new normal for the way my life is now. And appreciate it. Does it have to be going on a trip or learning a new hobby? Can my second-chance list have just one thing on it—to simply be?"

"That's a wonderful thing to want to be, Sherri," Lynn said. "You don't have to celebrate your end of treatment like any one of us. It's unique to you. April likes big gestures and new experiences. Your goal can be to live your life in the moment and enjoy it. There's no right or wrong answer."

Sherri smiled and leaned back in her chair. "I kept thinking I had to want something more."

April said, "You're not me, Sherri. You haven't traveled my road, so why should you want the same things? And maybe we'll end up at the same place, just from different directions."

The discussion thread was picked up by Gwen, who had been cancer-free for six years. Lily shared a funny story about one of her kindergartners remarking about how her bald head looked like his dad's. Lynn's eyes focused on April when a lull fell in the group. "What about you, April? Anything to share this week?"

"We've talked about how our treatments help us to get better. To destroy the bad cells in our bodies. Talking about getting better gives us hope and something to hold on to when we're losing our lunch in the bathroom. That one day, this will all end." She paused and realized again how much she appreciated this group of tough women. "I've gotten to know someone recently who has a disease that will never get better. Watching her son take care of her and knowing there is no cure breaks my heart." Her voice cracked, and she paused again to control her inner turmoil.

"What I've gone through with breast cancer made me take a long look at my life, and I didn't like what I saw. If there's anything positive about this, for me, it's that I'm a better person because of it." A tear slipped out of the corner of her eye, and she wiped it away with her pinkie finger. "It would have been great if it didn't take cancer to wake me up, but that's what happened. And I'm thankful for every day since my diagnosis."

Others nodded and Sherri reached over to pat her on the shoulder. Lynn sucked in a deep breath and released it. "Thank you for sharing that." She had them stand and join hands. They finished the meeting with an affirmation of healing.

Sherri followed April to her car. "What you said in there was beautiful."

"It's been on my mind lately, while watching Zach with his mom." She toyed with her car keys as she tried to find the right words. "She will never get better, and he loses a piece of her with each minute that goes by.

But, I was given a second chance. And I'm going to grab it with both hands."

Sherri nodded and gave April a hug. "Me, too."

CHAPTER EIGHT

DR. FRAZIER'S OFFICE number popped up on her phone as April stood in the home improvement store staring at cans of paint. She put the basket full of painting supplies on the floor and answered the phone. "Iris, what's going on? The nurses have you calling your own patients these days?"

Dr. Frazier cleared her throat on the other end. "I need to see you in my office as soon as you can make it. I'd like to go over your test results."

"Well, I'm off work today. Are you available in five minutes?" She chuckled, but the silence on the doctor's side made her pause. "It's that serious?"

"There's something in your blood work from last week that has me very concerned."

Oh. The store suddenly felt ten degrees warmer, and April clawed at the scarf that she'd tied around her neck and unzipped her jacket. "Is the cancer back?"

"You know there are certain markers in the blood that I keep an eye on. One of them is really elevated."

"But it could be nothing."

"Or it could be something we need to get a better look at."

That meant more tests. An MRI and a PET scan. Maybe even a mammogram to see if the breast tissue that remained had developed cancer. She couldn't do this again. Wouldn't be able to fight. She'd thought this was all over with. Thought she'd put this in her past. She was working through her second-chance list because she was healthy again. She was supposed to be picking out a new paint color for her bedroom, not worried about more tests to tell her if the cancer had returned.

She swallowed. "When do you want me to come in?"

"Now."

April abandoned the basket of supplies in the aisle and drove to the medical building beside the hospital. She waited in the lobby until one of Dr. Frazier's nurses came to get her. Instead of putting her in an examination room, the nurse escorted her to Iris's personal office. April entered and took a seat in front of Iris and her massive oak desk. "This isn't supposed to happen. You said we got all the cancer out. I'm almost at my one-year marker. This isn't supposed to happen."

Dr. Frazier held out the file for April to peruse. "Read the results yourself. It might not be cancer, but I'd rather rule it out than just dismiss it, wouldn't you?"

April examined the file and sighed. "If this was my patient, I'd send her for a scan, at least. If only to rule it out." She groaned and tossed the file onto the desk. "Now I know how Page felt when you told her it was back."

"I'm not saying it's back yet."

April gave a decisive nod. She knew what had to be done. "So let's schedule that MRI and PET scan. And probably a mammogram to be safe."

Dr. Frazier crooked one of her eyebrows. "This is why I don't like doctors as patients. They think they know more than me."

"Do you disagree?"

"No, you're right." Dr. Frazier handed her

a sheet of paper with a prescription for the test. "Let's start with a PET scan to narrow our search."

"Great." April folded the paper and stuffed it into her purse. "Gut feeling, what do you think it is?"

"It's one marker, so I'm not too worried. But I want to be positive that it's not cancer."

"And if it is?"

"Then we'll deal with it." Dr. Frazier's practicality did little to buoy her spirits.

April sat with the receptionist as she called to set up the time for the test to be done. She left the office feeling as if she'd been wrung out like a washcloth. The excitement she'd had while choosing paint chips had fled with the phone call.

She pulled out her cell and searched her contacts. Her mom answered on the first ring. "April, honey, I was just thinking of you."

"Mom, where are you?" It sounded like she was in the middle of a construction zone with sounds of saws and hammering.

"I finally convinced your dad that we needed to remodel the kitchen." The background sounds got softer. "I moved to the bedroom. Can you hear me better?"

"Yes. Are you sitting down?"

Her mom agonized in her ear. "That's how you started the conversation when you told me you had cancer. What is it now?"

April told her about how the results had come back and that new tests were planned as a result. "I'm scared, Mom."

"You beat it once. If, and it's a big *if,* that's what it is this time, then you'll beat it again."

Page would have smirked at her mother's response. Her mom was the original Mary Sunshine, espousing an optimism that she'd passed on to April along with her blond hair and blue eyes. "And Dr. Frazier didn't say that it was cancer. Just that she wanted to make sure it wasn't."

"I know. But I didn't think it was cancer last time, and it was. I won't be fooled again."

"You're not a fool for wanting to believe it's nothing. We'll believe it's not cancer until we're told otherwise."

That's why she'd called her mom first. She needed to believe that everything would be okay. "Thanks, Mom. We'll have to plan a weekend for me to come up and see you and Dad soon."

"You better."

They chatted about her dad's plan to retire in the coming years as well as her brother and his new girlfriend. They ended the conversation with a promise to talk in the next few days. April felt worlds better after finishing the call. Her mom was right. She'd believe it wasn't cancer, until Dr. Frazier confirmed if it was. And she was going to hang on to that word *if* for all it was worth.

ZACH'S CELL PHONE BUZZED, but he didn't spare it a glance. Instead, he highlighted a section of the contract on his computer screen and typed a question mark in the comments section. He needed to get the injury clause verified before he could allow his client to sign his life over.

A knock at the door, and Zach glanced up. Dalvin pointed to the phone. "Your mother's nurse on line four. She said she's been trying to reach you."

He didn't need another interruption in his jam-packed schedule, but he also didn't want to jeopardize losing another good caretaker. He picked up the receiver. "Dolores?"

"You need to come home."

Zach glanced at the pile of papers on his desk and checked his watch. "It's not even noon. Can't you handle whatever it is?"

"I wouldn't call you at your office if I could. Your mother is threatening to hurt herself if you don't come home."

He didn't need this. Not now. Not today. He loved his mother, but there were times when that love became a challenge, an overwhelming one. "Can it wait an hour?" Silence on the other end, and he cursed himself for sounding so unfeeling. "I need to clear some things up here and then I'll be right over. Tell her I'm on my way. Tell her I'm stuck in traffic. Just tell her what she wants to hear, and I'll be there as soon as I can."

He slammed the phone down harder than he had intended. He groaned and pushed his thumbs into the temples on his forehead. How long could he go on like this? Pressing the intercom button, he summoned Dalvin.

His assistant entered the office with his tablet and stylus, then shut the door behind him.

"Today is not a good day for your mother to have another meltdown."

"When is it a good time?" Zach started shoveling papers into his messenger bag. "I'm supposed to have dinner tonight with Lorelei and her father so that we could sign her contract. I should be able to make that if I can get my mother calmed down by then."

Dalvin scanned his tablet and shook his head. "That's tomorrow night. You have a meeting with the big boss Mike and the other agents at four this afternoon."

"Right. If I hurry home, I'll be back by then."

"And if Mike stops by to talk to you beforehand?"

Zach put his coat on and buttoned it while he tried to come up with an excuse besides the obvious one. "I'm checking out a potential client."

Dalvin raised one eyebrow at this. "That's what we used last week when you needed to duck out early. How many fictional clients are you scouting?"

"I don't know. Make something up."

Dalvin made a note on his tablet. "You should be paying me more."

"I agree. And when this chaotic mess with my mother settles down, we can discuss it."

"When do you think that will be?" He put a hand on his hip. "It's getting worse, not better. I've been covering for you as best I can, Zach, but our luck will eventually run out if you don't do something."

"Well, I haven't exactly been on a beach somewhere sipping piña coladas, Dalvin." Zach spread his arms out wide. "I can't just drop my mother off at a home and hope that she gets better. I'm responsible for her."

"Being responsible doesn't mean you do it on your own."

Zach gritted his teeth. He didn't need another lecture from someone who thought they knew better than he did. They weren't there every night when his mother's mercurial moods decided to come out and play. They didn't see the confusion and pain in her eyes when they put her to bed. They didn't lie in their bed and pray for peace just for one night. "I'll be back as soon as I can."

Dalvin colored slightly and put out a hand. "I didn't mean—"

"I know." Zach pushed past him and hurried out of the office.

OVER THE NEXT few days, April had all three tests, so there was nothing to do now but wait for the results. To distract herself, after work, April stopped at the home improvement store and picked out a soft lavender paint for her bedroom. It reminded her of the color of lilacs in spring, a sign of hope and renewal. Two things she needed at the moment.

She bought the paint, brushes, roller and various other tools. In her car, she called Page and asked if she wanted to come to a painting party if April supplied the pizza and chips. "As fun as that sounds, I have to be at the hospital tonight. Why this yearning to paint all of a sudden?"

"It's on my second-chance list. When I was sick, I remember staring at those four bedroom walls and longing to have a new color."

"Sunday's my day off. Could it wait until then?"

April sighed. "I guess it could." She paused.

"Dr. Frazier saw something in my blood work and sent me for more tests."

"No."

"Yes, she did. But for now my mom and I believe it's nothing." She waited for Page to say something else. "I'm sorry I wasn't more understanding when you told me that your cancer was back last year."

"What are you talking about? You were amazing. You said you'd take the cancer on yourself to spare me."

"Well, I didn't realize what it felt like for you."

"April, I love you to death. But you did nothing wrong." Page took a deep breath. "And I'll believe it's nothing along with you if it helps."

"Thanks. See you Sunday."

"No mushrooms."

"Fine."

IT TOOK A few days, but Zach was finally able to nail down a dinner date with April. He waited at the table, anxiously watching the door for April to enter. He'd invited her to dinner. She'd accepted, but warned him that she was coming straight from work after a twelve-hour shift so not to expect miracles with her appearance. He'd tried to reschedule for a more convenient time, but she insisted that she'd need a good meal after the day she was having.

She entered the restaurant and scanned the room, smiling when she saw him. He stood as she approached the table and held out a chair for her. He had to admit that she might look tired, but she was still beautiful with pink in her cheeks and a snap in her eyes. She sat down, and he took his seat across the table from her. "Everyone should look as good as you after a long stint at work."

She blushed even more. "You don't have to say things like that. I know what I look like." She reached up to touch her hair and pat it into place. "I've been looking forward to this dinner all day." After picking up the menu from the table, she perused it.

Zach already knew what he was ordering since he tended to get the same thing every time, but he lifted up his menu all the same and watched her over the top of it. "The chicken verde enchiladas are wonderful here."

She glanced at him briefly and nodded, but returned to the myriad of choices on the menu. Finally, she closed her menu and he did the same. Placing her napkin on her lap, she smiled up at him. "It was nice of you to do this for me."

"It's my pleasure. I appreciate all the help you've given me."

The waiter arrived, and after their orders were taken, Zach looked over at her. "So, how were things at the hospital?"

She rolled her eyes and moaned. "It's a full moon. I work in an emergency room. How do you think it went?"

She regaled him with a few stories of what she'd experienced, and he ended up chuckling loudly. "My bad days can't compare to yours."

"Oh, it wasn't bad. More an adventure."

"How do you do that? Turn bad situations into something akin to fun?"

She shrugged and smiled wider. "I grew up that way I guess. I'm just a positive person, even when things don't look so good."

"Is that how you got through your cancer treatment?"

"Don't get me wrong. There were some bad days, but that's why I wrote my second-chance list. I knew good days were coming, and I wanted to fill them with things that I've always dreamed of doing. Like going to New York."

"You've mentioned that before. What's stopping you?"

She fidgeted and rearranged her silverware before answering. "My doctor found something in one of my tests that concerns her. So now I'm in the middle of wondering what if. What if the cancer is coming back? What if it's not?" She peered up at him. "Do I put my life on hold while we figure this out, or do I make plans that might have to get canceled?"

"My opinion? Go for it. Book the trip. Even if the cancer is back, shouldn't you keep working on that list?" He took a deep breath. "Easy for me to say, though, when I'm in a holding pattern because of my mom. But if I had your independence? I'd be calling the airline and buying a ticket."

"You could, you know. Come with me."

"And what would happen with my mom? She needs me to take care of her."

"Even caretakers get to take a vacation every once in a while." She reached across the table and grabbed his hand. "I've seen what happens when a person makes the sick family member their whole world. They die along with the patient. You have family and nursing support that are there to give you a break, but you don't use them enough. You tell them and yourself that you can do it on your own. But you can't, and you know it."

He bristled under her criticism. She didn't know what it was like to put in a full day's work at the office then go home and do another full night caring for his mom. She had no clue what it was like to want to be able to run away for just a few days, to get a respite from responsibilities. Instead, she sat there and lectured him on it. He checked out the other customers, unable to meet her eyes for a moment. Trying to get his anger and frustration to dissipate. When he looked at her again, he shook his head. "I've been taking care of my mother for almost twenty years. So don't tell me what I can and can't do."

"Zach, I'm not saying that you don't take good care of her because you do. But the time is coming when you won't be able to do it no matter how much you want to. And in the meantime, you're running yourself ragged. Who's taking care of you?"

He cleared his throat. "Can we change the subject? I don't want our date to end in an argument."

She frowned at this. "We're on a date? I thought dinner was a show of gratitude."

The waiter chose that opportune moment to deliver their meals, and Zach thanked him for rescuing the conversation. He started to eat, but looked up from his plate to find April watching him. She raised one eyebrow. "This is a date?"

He nodded. "Our second, from my estimation. Third, if you want to count being at the wine tasting together. Granted, I didn't invite you to that, but it was like a date all the same."

"I thought you didn't date."

"I don't have time. But there's something about you that speaks to me, that drags me away from my routine life and makes me want to explore life differently."

He meant it as a compliment. But her eyes

blazed with a determination that made him want to wince.

"So come with me to New York."

"You know I can't."

"You just said that I make you want something different, so come with me. Let's explore the Big Apple together. We could go see a show. Walk through Central Park. Maybe catch a game at Madison Square Garden."

She gave him a dazzling smile, and he had to swallow the disappointment that he couldn't make this happen for her. "You're asking the impossible."

"But it is possible, if you would just let yourself accept help. To loosen that fist you clutch on to your mom with and let someone else take over for only a few days." She thumped the table with her fist. "Let's do this together."

He wished he could. He could see the two of them discovering New York City's treasures. Strolling hand in hand along Fifth Avenue. Eating dinner in Little Italy. Shopping at Saks. He could picture kissing her goodnight outside her hotel room before turning and walking into his own. He could imagine it, wanted it, but he couldn't do it. "No."

April's jaw set into a tight line. "Well, I'm doing it. Like you said, what's stopping me?" She picked up a taco and bit into it, letting the insides fall onto her plate and not caring if they did.

PAGE SAT BACK on her heels and dipped her brush into the can of paint. April made broad strokes of lavender with the roller. "You asked him to go with you?" Page asked.

"And he turned me down." Her voice was tinged with disappointment. Even she could hear it. She continued to fill the huge expanse of wall with the loveliest shade of light purple. "Can you believe that?"

"What I can't believe is that you expected him to drop everything and go with you. You barely know the guy."

"I know enough."

Page snorted and attacked the baseboards. "You're too impulsive, and you get upset when everyone else around you doesn't throw caution to the wind along with you."

"I've been cautious for far too long. It's

time for me to be more free-spirited." She stood back and admired her work before putting more paint on the roller. "If I asked you, would you have come with me?"

"Of course I would. Because I'm your best friend." Page paused and glared at her. "And why haven't you asked me?"

"Because you hate New York."

"I don't hate it. I just have bad memories of my last time there with Chad."

"Do you want to come with me? We could replace those bad memories with good ones." She smiled. "We could even throw in a day at the spa. We've always talked about doing that, but never found the time."

"Sounds tempting."

"But…"

Page stood and groaned as she put her free hand at the base of her spine and stretched. "These back pains are killing me. I should set up an appointment with a chiropractor. Or a massage therapist. I don't understand why I'm so old and feeble all of a sudden." She rested her paintbrush on the drop cloth and walked toward April. "I'd love to go. Let me talk to Joanne and see if I can use my vacation time. When are you planning on going?"

April squealed and hugged Page. "That would be amazing if you could go with me. In a few weeks. I'll check the dates. We are going to have so much fun. We won't even have time to sleep because our days will be so jam-packed with activities."

Page sighed. "I'm starting to regret this."

They returned to painting, the only sound in the room coming from the wireless speaker that played pop music. April sashayed to the rhythm. All the months she'd spent in her bed wishing to be well, staring at these four walls and imagining what it would be like to have the energy to change their color. To be able to use her arms and body fully. To feel alive and healthy enough to spend an afternoon painting and making her bedroom beautiful.

And if she faced chemo again, then she could look at these walls and remember when she'd felt good and know those days would come again.

NONNA HANDED HIM the bag of groceries and scolded. "You turned that poor girl down? What were you thinking?"

"I was thinking that I don't have the freedom to just leave and go off somewhere." He'd stopped at his grandparents' store after work to pick up some things before heading home for the night. "What would happen to my mom? I can't leave her."

"We've told you that we want to help as much as we can. Why don't you let us?"

"Because she doesn't remember you and that makes her upset."

Nonna looked away. He hated to hurt her by saying that, but it was the truth. His mom didn't remember her parents anymore. The last time they'd come over, she'd thought they were there to take her away. That they were putting her in a hospital to die. He'd begged his grandparents to leave then, and had spent the rest of the evening trying to calm down his mother. What would happen if they took over her care so he could fly to New York? His mother would think he'd abandoned her. He couldn't do that to her. Couldn't add to her confusion and frustration.

"And April is hardly a poor girl. She's strong enough to get over her disappointment in me." They walked to his car and put the groceries in the trunk. He turned to look at

Nonna. "She thinks that I should put Mom into a home."

Nonna nodded, considering his words. "Maybe it's time."

"You're giving up on her, too?"

"Is getting her the best care really 'giving up'? You won't be able to do it by yourself forever."

"I have nurses that come over."

"Soon that won't be enough."

He couldn't hear this from his grandmother, too. Bad enough that April tried to convince him that he should desert his own mother. "I can handle her just fine." He slammed the trunk down and went to the driver's side. "I can't put her in a home, Nonna. I just can't. And I wish everyone would stop pressuring me to do that. She's okay with me."

"No, she's not."

"It's the only way."

"You're wrong, and eventually, you'll understand that."

He shook his head and got into his car, slamming the door. He started the car and paused as Nonna returned to the store. She meant well. He knew that, but she didn't understand. Neither did April. He couldn't leave his mother. She needed him desperately.

He put the car in gear as he realized that part of him needed her, too.

THE WEBSITE FOR the hotel promised that it was located near the action of New York City. April clicked on the images of the lobby, the rooms, the views. She checked the map and found that it was in Midtown, within walking distance of much of what she hoped to see. Without hesitation, she clicked on the reservation button and started to fill out the information. Before she finished booking the room, she grabbed her cell phone and called Page. "I'm making the reservation right now. Are you coming?"

"Just tell me when."

April smiled and pressed the send button, confirming the reservation. She stood on the edge of marking another item off her list. "Well, start packing your bags because we leave in two weeks. We'll be there in time for Saint Patty's Day and the big parade."

"A big city full of drunks. Oh, joy."

Okay, so Page didn't sound nearly as ex-

cited as April felt, but she knew this would be
an epic trip. She searched the Broadway ticket
website to find what shows would be available during their stay. Most of the popular
ones were sold out but promised that same-
day tickets could be found when they arrived
in the city. Maybe she'd wait and try to get in
that way. "I also found a spa near the hotel
that sounds fantastic. Hot-stone massages.
Manis and pedis. Seaweed wraps. The whole
package."

"Whatever you want is fine with me. This
is for you."

"Is there anything you want to do while
we're there? It's not just my trip. We can ex-
orcise the ghost of Chad's ego easily. There's
so much to do."

She knew the story about how Chad had
turned their anniversary trip into a series of
job interviews. He'd decided that they would
move there and blamed Page when things
didn't go as planned. He'd abandoned her in
the middle of Central Park, where her purse
got stolen and she ended up having to trek
five miles to the hotel only to find herself

locked out and no Chad in sight. She'd sat in the lobby for five hours until he came back.

Page cleared her throat. "Anything we do will exceed that fiasco. Fill our days with as much stuff as you want to, and I will follow you."

"Isn't there one thing you wish you'd done?"

"Well…"

The way she paused before saying anything, April knew it had to be something good. Page relented. "Okay, fine. There's a place they show in the movies and on TV that has those giant cups of frozen hot chocolate. I'm not sure of the name of the place, but that's where I want to go."

"Really? You don't like chocolate."

"It's not that I don't like it, it's that too big a deal is made over it. But that frozen-drink thing looks really decadent. Delicious. For once, I want to be frothy and too sweet like that drink, okay?"

Two things that Page definitely wasn't. "Okay. I'll find the place." It was the least that April could do for her best friend and biggest supporter. "This is going to be amazing."

"Don't let your expectations get too high, or the city won't be able to live up to them."

Somehow, April doubted that this trip would lead to disappointment. She'd dreamed of going since she was a kid, and she was finally doing it. No more excuses. No more reasons not to. This was one item she was definitely marking off her list.

CHAPTER NINE

APRIL SWALLOWED THE bitter taste in her mouth as the plane landed at JFK. She glared at the empty seat next to her. Page would be arriving tomorrow due to a scheduling conflict at the hospital. April had argued that she would wait and postpone the trip, but her friend had insisted she go in time to see the Saint Patrick's Day parade. "That's something you don't want to miss. And I'll be there the next morning to go to the spa like we planned," Page had said.

So here she sat, alone, wondering how she would navigate the city on her own. The plane taxied to the gate and passengers unbuckled seat belts and began to fill the aisles. Everyone seemed anxious to get going. April sat, looking out the window at the airport. She wasn't in any hurry. The crowd could jostle in the aisles to leave a few minutes sooner.

Once the plane had emptied, April stood

and removed her carry-on bag from the overhead bin and walked to the door. One of the flight attendants smiled and welcomed her to New York. April returned the grin and made her way into the busy terminal. People didn't walk; they ran to their gates, to baggage claim, to the taxi stand. April strolled the halls and followed the directions to baggage claim, where she picked up her bright pink rolling suitcase. No mistaking that it was hers.

Arrows directed her to the taxi stand, and she waited in line for the next available cab to take her to the hotel. She gave the cabbie the hotel's name, then settled back into the seat. She couldn't take her eyes from the window, soaking in the sights and sounds of the city. She fished her cell phone out of her pocket and texted Page. Here at last. Wish you were with me.

She put her phone back into her pocket and marveled as they entered the busy traffic heading toward Midtown. She had a few hours before she'd need to walk where the parade would pass by. In her travel book, she'd found a deli on the parade route where she could eat lunch and enjoy the things from there.

The taxi arrived at the hotel, and she paid the cabbie before grabbing her suitcase. She stood outside the massive building and tilted her head back to get the entire piece of classic architecture into focus. She put a hand on top of her head to keep her stocking cap from falling off and grinned. She was hardly a country bumpkin making her first trip into the city. She'd had almost a decade to shed her small-town roots. Yet this was something truly special.

She entered the hotel through a revolving door and was greeted by a bellhop who tipped his cap to her before hurrying away with a cart full of luggage. She approached the front desk and waited while the receptionist helped the family in front of her. The little girl sucked on two of her fingers as she stared at April, who gave her a small wave. The girl frowned and buried her face in her mother's pant leg.

Okay, then. The family left the front desk, and April moved forward. She took out the printed confirmation from the hotel's website and her driver's license, placing both on the marble counter. The receptionist greeted her and entered the information into his computer. "I see you've upgraded to our VIP suite with two bedrooms." He looked up and waggled his eyebrows. "Very nice. Posh. Fabulous views. First-class all the way."

This couldn't be happening. "Your computer's wrong," she blurted, pointing to her paper with the confirmation. "I booked a room with no view and two queen-size beds. There's got to be some kind of mistake." It had been the best option that she could fit into her budget for the trip.

The clerk turned back to his computer and hit a few more keys. "No. VIP suite."

"I can't afford a suite." But she brought out the credit card under which she'd reserved the room and slapped it on the counter.

The receptionist slid the card back toward her. "It's paid in full."

"You put the suite on my card before I got here? What if I had canceled?" She was surprised the charge had gone through considering her limit.

"It's under a different card." More furious typing. "A Zachary Harrison paid for it."

That man! She closed her eyes and fought the urge to groan aloud. What had he done? He couldn't go with her, so he felt guilty and upgraded her reservation? She wondered what other surprises waited for her. She put her ID and credit card back into her wallet and stuffed it in her carry-on bag. "I'll only need one key for now. My friend won't be in until tomorrow."

After getting directions to her suite, she took the key and walked to the glass elevator, her suitcase rolling behind her. The up button had already been pressed, so she glanced around the spacious lobby while she waited. She shook off the anger at Zach's gesture and decided to enjoy it. After all, that was the point of the entire trip: to have a good time and live a little.

The elevator let her out on the top floor, and she crept down the hushed hallway to her suite. She slid the key card in and out of the lock, and slowly opened the door to reveal the most luxurious room she'd ever seen. Floor-to-ceiling windows showcased the New York skyline. Studying the view, a smile twitched her lips. She then turned and took in the fireplace, the silk-papered walls, the marble-tiled floor. Plush velvet sofas flanked the fireplace, and a wet bar waited on the other side of the room. Two doors off the living area led to two bedrooms, each with their own bathroom that had televisions set in the shower wall. King-size beds with thick comforters and at least a half dozen pillows.

Wow.

She got out her cell and sent a quick text to Zach. You didn't have to do this for me.

She paused a moment and then typed another message. Thank you.

ZACH'S CELL PHONE buzzed while he was on his office phone with a tennis coach who wanted to work with his client. The girl's father had recently fired the previous coach for being too soft on Lorelei, and the search for a new one had left Zach with a headache. The dad had a list of requirements a mile long, and no one was good enough. Didn't matter if the coach had taken his last two players to Grand Slam tournaments five years running.

He ended the call with a promise to give him a meeting with Lorelei and her dad in the following week. He put his feet on his desk and leaned back in his chair. While his client showed promise, the problem was her indomitable dad and his unattainable standards. Zach had already bought a bigger bottle of aspirin for the inevitable headaches.

Remembering he had a message on his cell, he picked the phone up from the desk and glanced at the screen. April had made it to the hotel and discovered his gift, then. He smiled and texted back. You're welcome. Enjoy NYC.

You should be here with me. You'd love it.

He poised his finger above the keyboard, debating how to respond. He may not be able to be there with her, but he could help her have a good time. See you when you get back.

Putting the phone away, he wondered how she'd like the other surprises he had planned for her.

THE WALK TO the parade route was a lot longer than it had looked in the guidebook she'd purchased before she'd left Detroit. It had seemed like only a couple of blocks, and she could walk it in a few minutes. But the real city blocks stretched farther. Good thing she'd joined the gym and had been working with her trainer to get in better shape.

After the parade, she lingered, glancing into the window displays of the stores that lined the streets. She entered a boutique with a bright pink sign and found it full of items designed for breast cancer survivors. April picked up a bracelet with the word *warrior* etched into it. It reminded her of Sherri, and she decided to get it for her friend. There was a T-shirt for Page that would definitely make her laugh. She took the purchases to the cash register where a woman with no eyelashes and a bald head was stationed. April held out her hand. "I'm April. Stage 3 breast cancer."

"Naomi. Stage 1B."

"They caught it early."

Naomi rang up the items. "I was lucky. My mom, not so much." She put the items in a white plastic bag that sported a pink ribbon. "I opened the store with my inheritance, not knowing that the same cancer would touch me, too."

"It's a wonderful tribute to her." April looked

at the framed picture on the wall behind the cash register. "She'd be proud of you."

"Actually she'd be angry I left my job at a big bank." Naomi gazed up at the picture of her mom. "But then, I usually disappointed her." She handed the bag to April. "Stay strong."

"You, too."

Since getting cancer, she'd met more survivors than she'd ever known before. It was like a sisterhood that drew women together, so she didn't feel so alone on this journey.

She returned to her hotel room and started the fireplace while she lay on the sofa and read the guidebook, trying to decide what to do next. Most of the items on her list were those she wanted to share with Page once she arrived tomorrow. The thought of going somewhere to get dinner made her feet ache, so she ordered room service and had her meal while sitting in front of the picture window, watching the city lights turn on.

BANGING ON HER hotel room door roused April from sleep. She squinted at the clock on the nightstand and groaned. She was on vacation, so she shouldn't have to get up at dawn. She pushed the sheets and blankets off her, then grabbed the hotel-supplied plush bathrobe before walking out into the living space. She wrapped the bathrobe's belt around her and tied it tight before peering through the peephole.

She blinked and looked again. Opened the door and squealed before throwing her arms around Page and then Sherri. "What are you doing here?"

Page rolled her eyes. "Your not-so-secret admirer sent us both on a red-eye flight." April stood aside so her friends could bring in their luggage. "He didn't want you to be alone on this trip."

Sherri whistled as she took in the view. "This is some place. I've never stayed in a room this fancy." She set her suitcase down and immediately headed for the window to get a better look at the city.

"We're going to have so much fun that New York won't ever be the same." April put an arm around Page's shoulders. "And we're starting with a day at the spa."

A few hours later, the three women lay

facedown on massage tables in a large room where floral scents drifted in the warm air. April had explained to their massage therapists about their cancer and the need to avoid touching certain areas. And because of her radiation treatments, Sherri couldn't have any oils applied to her skin.

April closed her eyes as the masseuse used his elbow to dig deep into the muscles between her shoulder blades. She clamped her lips together so she wouldn't moan. Even if it did feel incredible.

"We have to do this again when we get home," Page said as her masseuse kneaded her neck. "I used to make fun of Dr. Weber when she said she was going to get a massage after work, but I'm a total convert now."

"I don't know. Dez is pretty good at this, too," Sherri said from the other table.

April smirked. "Sure, rub it in that Agent Hottie is the total package when it comes to being a husband. Some of us aren't so lucky and are still single."

"I don't know. Zach seems to be pretty hung up on you."

"I'm not sure what he is." April closed her

eyes and thought of Zach. He'd referred to their last dinner together as a date, but he hadn't phoned her since. Hadn't invited her to do anything together. That was a week ago. And yet, he'd sent her friends here. Upgraded her hotel room. If anything, she was getting mixed messages from him. Did he want to be with her? Not want to be with her?

"What do *you* want *him* to be? That is the better question."

April rose up on one elbow and looked over at Sherri. "I want him to want to be a part of my life instead of giving me the reasons that he can't be. I want him to be present when we are together."

"You want him. Period." Page sighed. "I'm going to be the only single one left in our group, aren't I?"

"Zach and I are far from being a couple, so you can relax."

"But it's destined to happen between you two, isn't it?"

April didn't know how to answer. If anything, it felt less of a sure thing. In fact, there was nothing that made her think he would be with her. He'd made his stance about his mother very clear. She came first and to the exclusion of everything else. When he cared for his mother, he had room for no other woman in his life. While she might admire his dedication and devotion to his mom, she felt left out. "You're wrong. It's guilt that made him pay to upgrade the room and brought you both here. He couldn't be, so he sent you."

"I bet there's more going on than you think."

The massage therapists finished and left the room. April sat up and pulled the sheet around her. "He's made it very clear that he doesn't have time for a girlfriend."

"So convince him otherwise. Show him what he'd be missing out on if he let you get away."

"And what would that be? What can I offer him?"

"Are you kidding? You're a safe place to fall. Someone to turn to when the world gets to be too much and you need peace. You're sunshine on a rainy day." Page shrugged. "You've got more to give him than he could find anywhere else."

April raised an eyebrow at this. "You're exaggerating."

"So what if I am? You have a lot to offer, so don't sell yourself short. Don't tell yourself that you'll be okay when we both know that you're as into him as he is into you." Page slid off the massage table and walked over to April's. "You keep asking me why you're still single. I can tell you that it's because you downplay yourself. You are a strong, successful woman with a huge capacity for love. You are warm, genuine and funny. Any man would be lucky for you to love him and be in his life."

April hugged Page, wishing she was right about Zach. "I don't care what anyone says. You're a good person, Page. The best in my book. I'm the lucky one to have you as my friend."

Page gave her a quick squeeze, then stepped out of the embrace. "Don't get all sappy on me. You know how I am with that stuff."

Sherri joined the two of them, wrapped in a sheet and trying to keep a hold on the edges. "I feel like melted butter. What's next?"

April wriggled her eyebrows and gave them both a wide smile.

PAGE SIPPED FROM the straw that was buried in an extralarge cup of frozen hot chocolate with mounds of whipped cream and chocolate sprinkles. April took a picture of her on her cell phone and posted it on Instagram before her friend could object. "People we work with will see that," Page said as she tried to take the cell phone away.

"Exactly. No one will believe that Nurse Grumpypants actually enjoyed something decadent."

Sherri stirred her own drink. "Nurse Grumpypants?"

Page rolled her eyes. "Don't ask."

"It's a nickname that one of the ob-gyns gave her a long time ago because of her gloomy disposition. It's kind of stuck ever since." April had a taste of her hot chocolate and put her mug down, feeling the whipped cream on the tip of her nose. She crossed her eyes to see if it was there.

Sherri snapped a picture and held the cell phone away when April attempted to grab it.

"Fair play and all." She laughed and set her cell phone back on the table after she'd posted the photo. "Dez isn't going to believe this."

"I'm surprised Agent Hottie could cope without you." April made embarrassing kissing noises.

A dreamy look passed over Sherri's face. "He said it was the least I should get after all the treatments I've had." She rested her cheek against her fist. "He knew he could trust me with the two of you in the Big Apple."

"That was his first mistake." Page grinned and handed April a napkin to wipe the whipped cream off her nose. "We are known troublemakers in Detroit. We're supposed to behave just because we left town?"

"Don't give Sherri the wrong impression. We're not hooligans." April paused, then flashed Page a wicked grin. "Remember when we used to tip over the new interns?" She turned to Sherri. "Page was notorious for walking next to someone crouched down to get medical supplies from a bottom shelf and giving them a shove to topple them."

"It wasn't a shove. More like a tap."

"Either way, they went down." April giggled. "The chief had to transfer her out of the ER so that the interns wouldn't quit."

"I wasn't the only one who tipped interns. You were just as guilty."

"Is that how you met? Working together?" Sherri asked.

She and Page both nodded. "The saddest day was when she transferred to Labor and Delivery. I no longer had a partner in crime in my department. The nurses now are more serious. Nothing like Page."

Sherri motioned to Page. "I would never have guessed that about you."

Page shrugged. "This was BC. Before cancer. I'm not as much fun as I used to be." She took another long sip of the frozen hot chocolate. "This here is worth the whole trip to New York for me. It doesn't matter what else we do. Nothing will top this moment."

SOMEONE KNOCKED ON Zach's open office door. Standing there was the owner of the agency. "You have a minute?" Mike asked.

Zach stood and motioned to a chair. "As many as you need."

Mike entered and shut the door. That

couldn't be a good sign, right? His boss walked to one of the windows that looked out onto the Detroit skyline. "You earned this office by bringing in big names and signing clients who have made us a lot of money." He turned to face Zach, then approached the desk and took a seat across from him. "You established our presence in a competitive field and made us the premier sports agency in the state."

"Why do I feel like there's a *but* coming?"

"The Zach I know was the first to arrive and the last to leave. You gave a hundred and ten percent every day."

"I still do."

Mike studied him over his glasses. "I've heard that you lost the next top tennis pro because you were unavailable to interview new coaches. In fact, Lorelei's father called me personally to tell me why his daughter was leaving our representation."

Zach swallowed and nodded. "That's true. I did have to cancel some of the interviews because of a personal problem."

"I know all about that. You've left early twice this week already because of that problem. And you missed our meeting this past Monday for the same reason."

"Are you firing me, sir?"

Mike laughed as if that was funny even if Zach couldn't find the humor in it. "I'm not firing you, but I am suggesting you take a leave of absence."

Zach shot to his feet and put his hands on his desk. "I assure you, sir, that I'm fine. I can take care of my personal issues outside of my commitments here. There's no need for me to be suspended."

"Suspended?" Mike frowned. "I'm talking about a leave to take care of your mother. Use some vacation time to find the help she needs so you can come back here with your full focus. I can't afford for you to drop another ball."

Zach's cell phone started to ring. He glanced at the number and pressed Ignore. "It's just my mother's nurse."

Mike sighed and got to his feet. "That just proves my point."

"I'm your number one agent."

"You were my number one agent, but Leslie is outperforming you this month, and Eric isn't far behind." Mike leaned forward on the desk. "Effective immediately, you're on vacation until further notice. Take care of your family, then come back stronger than ever. I need you, Zach. Don't let me down. Because the next time we have a conversation like this, I will fire you."

"I have appointments scheduled tomorrow."

"You can reschedule when you're back in two weeks, or another agent will be happy to see them."

"They know me, so they're expecting me. You know as well as I do that this business is all about relationships."

"Then let's go over what you have planned and make some calls."

Together, they dismantled Zach's entire schedule. He called clients and potential clients to reschedule. Assured clients on his roster that he would be back after a short vacation. His newest client and newlywed Chris expressed surprise, but Zach quickly reassured him. "You can still reach me by cell if something comes up. Your contracts are signed and delivered, so I don't anticipate anything will come up until I return."

Chris was silent on the other end, then he let out a long breath. "You'd tell me if something was wrong, wouldn't you?"

"I promised you honesty. I just need some time to take care of a few personal things."

Chris seemed satisfied with that, and he hung up sounding better than he had when the conversation had started. Mike went to the door and opened it. Before he stepped through, he turned and looked at Zach. "I don't want to lose you, but I need to do what's best for my company."

"Understood."

A few seconds after Mike left, Dalvin darted into the office. "He didn't give me a chance to buzz you and let you know he was coming in. What did the big boss want?"

Zach grabbed his coat and his phone. "To tell me I'm on vacation as of right now."

Dalvin's eyebrows disappeared into his hairline. "For how long?"

"Don't know. He mentioned two weeks, but my clients can't afford me to be MIA that long." He put his laptop into his messenger bag. "You know how to get a hold of me if anything comes up, right?"

"What am I supposed to do without you?"

"I hear Leslie is pretty busy with clients. She might appreciate your assistance."

Dalvin made a face. "She's so fake, that Leslie. If she's bringing clients into the agency, then it's because she's telling them what they want to hear."

"That's part of an agent's job."

"You never lie or mislead. You ask your clients what they want, then hustle to make it happen." Dalvin cocked his head to the side. "I'll miss you. Don't stay away too long."

"I won't know what to do with myself if I'm gone longer than a few days." Zach gave a laugh, but he meant it. He'd put in long hours at the office, then gone home to do the same. The thought of not having work to distract him from the situation with his mother gave him a headache. He shook Dalvin's hand. "I'll see you soon."

Dalvin sniffed and nodded. Zach hustled out quickly, trying to ignore the looks of the other agents and assistants. Especially Leslie, who gave him a smile and a finger wave.

She shouldn't get too comfortable being the top agent for the month. Because he'd be back better than ever like Mike had said.

In the parking garage, he sat in his car and wondered what he was supposed to do now. It was still early afternoon, and the thought of going home and dealing with whatever crisis Dolores had called him about made his stomach hurt. He rested his forehead on the steering wheel, closing his eyes.

His phone buzzed, and dreading what he'd see, he took it from his pocket and checked the screen. Not Dolores, but April. Having a fabulous time here in NYC. But you should be with me.

Ironically, if he didn't have his mother, he'd be hopping on a plane and flying out to meet her. But the reality of his life didn't allow him to be spontaneous. Instead, he texted her back, Wish I could. Before he lost his nerve, he sent a second message. Miss you.

Bubbles appeared on his screen, making him smile. Miss you, too. We should talk when I get home.

His smile disappeared. Why did women always want to talk? Couldn't they accept that he couldn't give as much as they wanted? That he had responsibilities that meant they would never be his only priority? But he swallowed all this. Can't wait.

WHEN THEY RETURNED to the hotel suite after their time at the spa, an envelope lay on the carpet just inside the door. Page reached down and picked it up, but handed it to April. "It's for you."

April shrugged and opened the envelope. Tickets for a musical for which she hadn't been able to get seats online. She noticed the seat numbers and whistled. "Anyone up for one of the hottest shows on Broadway?"

Page reached over and plucked the tickets out of April's hands. "Those are impossible to get. How did he do it?"

"He's an agent, so I'm sure he's got connections."

"What does a musical have to do with sports?" Page asked. "I think he's working a little too hard to win you over."

"There's nothing to win."

Sherri nodded. "Because you're already falling for him."

"We're friends, and he's hinted about something more. But that's all there is." When Page and Sherri gave her a look that meant they weren't buying it, April took the tickets back and stared at them. "Believe what you want, but he won't let me in close enough to feel anything. He's got another woman in his life."

"His mom doesn't count," Sherri said.

"She does though, because he will choose her every time." She headed for the bedroom, but turned back to her friends. "I'd be foolish to fall for him, right?"

Page seemed to be deep in thought, her expression serious. "Sherri's right. You're already falling and it scares you because it is crazy. But then, what love affair isn't?"

ZACH SHOWED UP to find Dolores sitting on the sofa, reading a magazine, while screaming came from his mother's bedroom. He put his messenger bag on the dining room table. "What is going on?"

He started down the hall when Dolores called after him, "I wouldn't go in there if I was you."

He shook his head at her suggestion, but when he opened his mom's bedroom door, his jaw dropped. The room no longer looked as it had. Furniture had been upturned. The sheets and blankets lay in a tangle on the floor. Clothes from her closet had been pulled out and thrown around the room. He took a step inside and reached out to stop her from making more of a mess. "Mom, stop yelling!"

She turned and slapped him hard across the face. He staggered back, and she rushed at him, hitting and scratching. He put his hands up to protect his head. Dolores must have heard the commotion and ran into the room. She put her arm straight out to fend off his mom while she helped him to recover his balance. Together, they backed out of the room and shut the door, leaving his mother on the other side.

Zach looked at Dolores. "What happened? I've never seen her like that."

"I've called an ambulance."

"What? No." What was a paramedic going to do? "She just needs some time to calm down."

"I called you earlier to tell you that she

was extremely upset. But what I just saw? It's escalated, and neither you nor I can control her." Dolores checked the scratch on his cheek. "She really got you."

He waved off her attention. "I'm fine. No big deal."

"Zach, she needs more help than we can give her. She needs to be in the hospital."

"No. We need to adjust her medication or something." He couldn't, no wouldn't, send her away. "This has happened before, and the doctor gives her something to help her."

"She's getting beyond what I can do. I can't come here anymore." Dolores turned on her heel.

He couldn't make this work if Dolores quit. He followed her. "You can't leave me. What will I do without you?"

Dolores set her mouth in a tight line, and her eyes filled with tears. "I don't know, but I can't help her anymore. She's getting too dangerous."

"She's an old woman. How is she dangerous?"

Dolores pointed to his reflection in the glass cabinet. It looked like he'd been in a bar fight, a bruise on one cheek and scratches down the other with more along his neck. She must have gotten a good shot at one of his eyes because it looked swollen. "You might be in denial about all this, but I'm not. I'll tell the agency that you need a different day nurse. However, after they ask me why, they may not be willing to send anyone else."

"Please, Dolores. I'll pay you extra. Whatever you want. Just don't quit on me. Please."

Dolores jerked her coat on and grabbed her purse. She stopped and put a hand on his shoulder. "It's time to admit that you can't take care of her anymore."

A loud shriek followed by a crash filled the air. Zach glanced toward the sound, and when he turned back to Dolores, she had already opened the back door to leave. He closed his eyes and fisted his hands at his sides.

Another crash came from his mother's room and then silence. He opened his eyes. The quiet stretched, and he strode down the hall and opened the bedroom door. His mother lay across the bed, a sleeve of her nightgown ripped and showing a red gash. She appeared to be asleep.

Zach ran to the bed and gathered her in his arms. "Mom, what have you done to yourself?" He checked the wound and found that it was deeper than he'd first thought. She'd need stitches at least. Further examination revealed a bump on her head.

A knock at the front door announced the paramedics. He gently laid her on the bed and left the room so he could let them in the house. "She's back here."

He brought them to the bedroom, then stood back so that they could care for his mom. One of the paramedics looked over at him. "Can you tell us how this happened?"

"She had a fit and threw things around the room. She's got Alzheimer's."

"Seems like she got in a few licks at you."

"I'll be fine. She's the one who needs help."

They checked the wound on her arm and flashed a penlight in her eyes. One of the EMTs left the room and returned with a stretcher. "We're going to take her to Detroit General so they can stitch her up and check her out."

He nodded and stood aside as they loaded her into the back of the ambulance. How he wished April would be in the ER waiting for them. She'd take care of his mom and know the right things to do to help her.

Because Zach sure didn't know anymore.

APRIL HATED TO leave New York, but real life waited for her back home in Detroit. Everything about her trip had been fantastic from the Broadway show they'd seen to the restaurants they'd eaten at to the long walk they'd taken in Central Park. Her second-chance list had gotten smaller as she'd marked off items one after another.

She'd texted Zach last night to thank him for everything he'd done to make her trip memorable, but he'd never responded. As she and her friends waited to board the plane, she checked her phone one more time. Still no answer.

She sipped her coffee to mask her disappointment and glanced at Page, who fidgeted in her seat. "Are you okay?"

Page grimaced, "It's my back."

"You need to get that checked out." When her friend didn't say anything, April peered at her closely. "I know that look. What is it?"

"I didn't want to say anything and ruin our trip."

"Well, we're about to head home, so you might as well tell me."

Still, Page didn't say anything. April motioned Sherri over from her seat. "Will you help me with something?" She positioned Sherri in the seat next to Page, then took the one on the other side of her. She took Page's hand in hers and had Sherri do the same. "We've got you on both sides now. We'll hold you up, okay? But you need to tell us what's going on."

Page hung her head, but squeezed April's hand. "You're a real pain in the neck, you know?"

Sherri nudged Page. "It's okay. You can tell us."

Page looked at Sherri first, then April. "Ovarian cancer."

Sherri covered her mouth with her free hand, but didn't let go of Page's. April nodded and let the doctor side of her take over because the friend side was close to losing it. "The back pain makes sense now. How far along?"

"Not sure yet."

"What's the plan?"

"Chemo followed by surgery to remove both ovaries."

"Both?"

Page gave a wry smile. "Because of my history, they're not taking any chances." She glanced between both women. "Third time's the charm, right?"

April took a deep breath and whispered, "Why didn't you say anything?"

"I'm saying it now."

"Oh, Page." April wrapped her arms around her best friend, and Sherri joined in the group hug.

They clung to each other until the gate attendant announced their flight was boarding. Page stood first and wiped her face with her hands. "Let's go home."

CHAPTER TEN

AFTER NEW YORK, going back to work felt like a letdown. April had been living on adventure and fun for three days, so returning to sutures and chest X-rays made life feel smaller. She tucked away her memories and kept her mind focused on her work.

Her second day back, she got called into one of the trauma rooms. Zach's mom smiled from the hospital bed when April entered the room, and asked, "Are you here to fix my hair?"

Based on the fact that Zach held a bloody dish towel to his mom's forehead, she needed more than a hairbrush to fix the problem. April walked to the opposite side of the bed from where Zach stood and tilted his mom's face toward her. She had Zach remove the towel and winced at the gash. "What's this?"

"She slipped and banged her head on the edge of the dresser."

April noticed the dark smudges under Zach's eyes. "She's starting to hurt herself?"

He wouldn't look at her. "We were here in the ER when you were in New York, too. She got stitches for a cut on her arm."

April nodded and returned her focus to his mom. "What happened to your head?"

Mrs. Harrison shrugged and reached up to touch the wound. "I don't know." She stared at Zach. "What happened, Robert?"

The nurse brought in a suture tray, and April sent her for saline. "I'm going to clean the wound first before I stitch it up, but you'll have to keep an eye on it to avoid infection."

"I know."

"I'm sure you do."

Zach allowed room for the nurse's return, and April got to work with the antiseptic. After the stitches, April used gauze to protect the wound. Removing her plastic gloves, she motioned for Zach to join her in the hallway. He shook his head. "You can say what you want in there. She won't understand us."

He clenched his jaw before she said a word. She knew that he understood what was coming since he'd probably heard this lecture last week when he'd had to bring his mother in. "I've closed up the gash in her forehead, but her problems are bigger than bruises and cuts. I want one of our doctors to evaluate her mental state before you go."

"No."

April moved closer, only inches away from him. "Zach, you can't keep doing this. You can't take care of her and ignore the other issues. She's deteriorating to the point where you can't protect her from herself."

"She's not trying to hurt herself. They're all accidents."

"But they keep happening." She tried to look him in the eye, but he had turned his face away from her. "I know you don't want to hear this, but you need to investigate long-term care facilities."

His eyes held hurt and anger. "No."

"Yes, you do. Otherwise, these emergency room visits are going to escalate until she seriously harms herself or you. And if you're not around, who will she have then?"

He pointed a finger in her face. "Don't start with me. You don't know what I'm going through."

"Maybe not." When his head dropped, she took his hand and squeezed. "But listen, Zach, I'm not telling you to abandon her in some hospital somewhere. I'm encouraging you to discuss this with a doctor to get her the care and attention she needs. She's outgrown what you can do for her." She turned Zach's body so that he had to look at his mother. "Is this how you want to see her?"

His expression crumpled, and he put his hands over his face. "No."

"Then let someone take over for you. You can't keep going down this road that you're on without damaging her or yourself."

"I'm a bad son."

April put her arms around him. "No, you're not. You're a good son for loving her and wanting to help her. But she's beyond you now." She rested her cheek on his chest. "It's only going to get worse if you don't do something."

"I can't handle any worse."

"So let me call one of our specialists in to evaluate her."

Zach pushed her away and walked to his mother's bedside. He didn't look at April as he got his mom's coat and helped her into it. "We're through here."

"Zach, please let us take care of her."

"You've done enough. She's stitched up. She's calm now. I'm taking her home."

"Why do you have to be so stubborn?" She blocked his path. "I could call adult services and have them come out to your house. Based on today's injuries and what you told me about last week, they have a case to remove her from your care. Is that what you really want?"

He glared at her. "I want you to leave us alone."

She tried to not let his words hit their mark, but her heart still ached at them. When he walked forward with his mom, she paused a moment in the doorway. "You're making a big mistake."

"Then let me make it."

He passed by her, his arms around his mother as they left the emergency room. April knew that despite what he said, it would hurt more to watch his mother deteriorate further. It would tear at him until he questioned everything he did and didn't do.

She was trying to save him from himself, if nothing else. She'd seen it a hundred times, adult children wanting to act as an advocate for their aged parent's care, refusing to take the advice of medical professionals because it meant admitting that they couldn't do everything. She'd watched as their own health worsened along with their parent's as they poured everything they had into coping. Not living. She didn't want to see this happen with Zach, but it seemed as if he was determined to follow that inevitable path.

She turned and glanced at the empty room, took a big breath and pushed down her emotions so she could handle the next patient.

ZACH SETTLED HIS mom into her bed and covered her with the comforter. She reached up and touched his cheek. "You look after me so well."

"I'm trying, Mom. Why don't you take a nap and then we'll have some lunch?" He kissed her forehead and took a seat in the recliner. He'd watch over her until he was sure she fell asleep.

That had been his mistake last night. He'd

read a chapter to her, then left her bedroom before assuring she was fully asleep. He'd gone to bed himself right after, so tired from taking care of her on his own. He'd woken to screams. She must have stayed awake and tried to rearrange the furniture in her bedroom. When she couldn't move the dresser, she'd beat on it first with her hands, since they were bruised, then with her head. He'd rushed in to find her doing this.

He'd tried to stop her, but she'd pushed him. For someone so seemingly frail, she'd been strong enough to flatten him. The only thing that had calmed her was his talking to her like his father had. Using pet names and phrases that Zach remembered him saying. Then she'd stopped and stared at him with unfocused eyes, muttering his father's name.

As much as he'd wished that April had been in the ER waiting for them on their first visit, he'd dreaded seeing her this last time.

But she was right. These few days at home with his mother had been brutal. He'd barely slept since he used her nap times to get things done that he couldn't handle otherwise. They had gotten close to running out of food, but he couldn't leave her alone to go shopping. He'd paid a premium price for a local store to drop off items. Nonna had scolded him, saying she would gladly have brought something to him. But he couldn't upset his mom further. Wouldn't let his grandmother see the condition she'd deteriorated to.

His pride was going to kill them both.

His mom stirred in her bed, and he broke off his thoughts to concentrate on her. If she were lucid, what would she want? Would she want to go to a nursing home when she was still so young? Or would she want to stay in the house that she knew and loved? Would she encourage him to get help for her or beg him to be the one to do it himself? He bounced back and forth between both positions.

She was his mom. He loved her and had taken care of her for so long. What would life without her being his focus be like? It excited and terrified him at the same time.

When he was sure that his mom was indeed asleep, he rose from the recliner and walked to the bedroom door. He kept the door open so that he could get to her sooner if he needed to. He'd learned that lesson, as well.

Once he was in the living room, he removed his cell phone from his pocket and dialed the number before he could stop. When she answered, he gulped in a big breath. "You're right. I can't keep doing this. Can you come over? I do need help."

Nonna arrived with a lasagna and a bag of cookies. She handed both to Zach. "Three seventy-five for forty-five minutes. You look like you could eat."

He put the lasagna in the oven, filled the kettle with water and put that on the burner to boil. He joined his grandmother at the dining room table. She folded her hands in front of her. "You might as well tell me everything." When he opened his mouth to object, she held up a finger. "Everything, bambino. I can't help you if I don't have the whole picture. And I know you've been keeping things from us."

So he told her. Over cups of hot tea and Italian cookies, he told her about the trips to the emergency room. How he'd been put on leave at work. His fears that the violence his mother was showing seemed to be heightening. "I don't even know where her anger is coming from."

His grandmother placed her mug on the table. "She's in a world that she doesn't recognize anymore. Wouldn't you be angry and scared?"

"I guess." He took a deep breath to stop the moisture in his eyes from building. "I don't want to lose her."

Nonna got up and came over to him to put her arms around him. "I understand, *caro*, I do."

When he'd finally spent his tears, he led her down to the bedroom to show how they'd been living. His mother turned over onto her side, and the bandage on her forehead stood stark white against her skin. Nonna gasped and put a hand to her mouth. "She looks older than I do."

"It's the disease. And the fact that I can only get her to sleep if I medicate her." He pushed his mother's stringy hair away from her eyes. He'd need to bathe her soon, a task he'd never thought he'd have to do for his mother. But then there were many things that she needed him for, mundane duties that he did because she no longer could. "She barely eats anything."

"What does her doctor say?"

"To keep her on the medication she's on. We've adjusted it a few times when she gets more confused, but I doubt it's working anymore."

"Have you thought of a second opinion?"

He pulled the blanket over his mother's shoulders. "April recommended someone, but it feels like we're past that point now."

"What have you got to lose?"

They watched his mom sleep peacefully for a few minutes longer. Back in the dining room, Zach cleaned up the mugs and plates from their snack and placed them on the counter, since the sink was already full. He knew that he should wash them, but he hadn't had time. And when he'd had time, he'd fallen asleep while surfing the internet to find answers about his mom's care. He turned on the faucet and squeezed liquid soap over the dishes already in the sink. He took out a dishcloth, and Nonna grabbed a towel. "You wash, I'll dry," she told him.

He washed a glass and handed it to her.

She dried it slowly and put it away in the cupboard. "Have you seen April lately?"

"She's the one who stitched Mom up this morning. And lectured me about not being able to take care of her." He thrust his hands into the warm, soapy water. "She also said she'd call adult services on me if I didn't get help."

"So that's why you called me."

"The thing is that she's right. You're right. Dolores was right. Everyone is saying that I can't keep going on like this, but I don't know what else to do. I can't just ditch her in some nursing home and forget her."

"Do you honestly believe you'd do that? I can see that she's become a burden, but you would never abandon her."

"Nonna, she was a burden when I was a teenager and I had to forgo after-school activities so I could come home and make sure she was okay. She's passed that. She's a weight around my neck that's going to eventually drown me." He handed her a dripping plate, but kept his hold on it. "Sometimes I hope she'll slip away in her sleep, and I'll be free. What kind of son am I?"

APRIL NEGOTIATED BETWEEN the rows of bicycles, stopping in front of one that had a frame the color of a fresh peach. She put a hand on the handlebars and told the salesperson, "This is it."

"But I haven't told you the features of this particular model." And the salesperson launched into a spiel on how this bike performed.

She nodded at the right places as he continued, but she'd made the decision to purchase it when she'd seen its cheerful color. She could be happy on a bike this shade of orange. She'd be fast and content to ride to work and through the neighborhood on a peach bike. When the salesperson finished talking, she tapped the handlebars. "I'll take it."

She paid for her purchase, and the clerk helped her cram it into the back seat of her car. She took it home and marked off "buy a bike and commute to work" from her second-chance list. It had been years since she'd ridden a bicycle, but that old saying existed for a reason, right? She'd be zipping around in no time.

Her cell phone buzzed, and she paused her

daydream of winning the Tour de France to answer it. "Dr. Frazier, I hope this is good news."

"Your test results from the PET scan and MRI indicate that there's nothing to worry about. The cancer markers in your blood were an anomaly."

April let out a puff of air. "Thank goodness. Do you know what caused it?"

"Can't say for sure. We'll keep an eye on it going forward, but right now our goal is to continue treatment with your current meds. I'll schedule you for more blood work and tests in three months."

After hanging up with her doctor, April took a seat on the sofa. She was still in remission. Cancer-free. She'd be okay.

She dialed Page's number. "My test results came back negative."

"That's great news, April. We should go out and celebrate."

"Are you sure you're up to that? How are you feeling?"

"Chemo starts next week, how do you think I am? I need a distraction, and a night out with you sounds perfect."

"You'll get to where I am someday. I know you will."

"Whatever. Pick me up at seven."

She hung up the phone and stared at her screen. She found his name and pressed it before she could talk herself out of it. It rang several times before he answered, sounding groggy. "Yeah?"

"Zach, it's April. Did I wake you?" She glanced at the clock on her DVD player. It was three in the afternoon. "Are you okay?"

"Just a sec."

April waited for a few minutes, then he was back on the other end of the phone. "I had to go in and check on my mom."

"How's she doing?" She hated to hear how exhausted he sounded. His voice soft and plaintive. His speech slow.

"Better. She's sleeping."

"How are you doing?"

There was a pause. "Why did you call me?"

Best to get to the point, she guessed. "I heard from my doctor, and I'm okay. It's not cancer."

"That's excellent, April. I'm happy for you."

She thought about what she was going to say, then just plowed through it. "I didn't mean to upset you about the care you're giving your mom. You're doing your best, really. I'm just worried that it's not enough."

"You're right, it isn't. But I'm not sure what to do next." He took a deep breath. "I take that back. I do know, I just don't want to do it."

"I can suggest some things, if you'll let me. I know people."

"I know you do." He yawned, and the silence stretched between them. Finally, he said in a soft whisper, "I miss you."

She smiled at this. "I miss you, too."

There was a sound in the background. "I have to go. Talk to you later."

And then he was gone. She looked at the phone and sighed. It was a start.

APRIL TOOK HER bike out of the garage and walked with it to the end of her driveway. She straddled it, sat up in the seat and pushed off. Pedaling past a few driveways, she had the bike making jerky movements until she found her sweet spot and darted down the road toward the hospital. She had a moment or two where the proximity of the cars to her felt a little too close for comfort, but she made it to the parking lot and arrived at work with time to spare.

She locked her bike in the racks near the entrance to the hospital and removed her helmet before heading into the emergency room. Janet waved from the reception desk. "Nice bike."

"Thanks."

April glanced at the duty roster on the nurse's computer and made notes of the staff who'd be alongside her in the department that day. She entered the locker room to store her possessions and hang up her coat. She found Kenny, a night shift doctor, resting on the sofa. He stood and greeted her with open arms. "It's been a full moon kind of night. I'm so happy you're here because I am going home and falling into bed for the next several hours."

"Appreciate that, Kenny."

"Two more weeks, and we get to switch. I'm counting down the seconds." He handed her his tablet. "Waiting on test results for two of the exam rooms. Broken jaw in trauma four waiting to be wired. And I ordered a psych consult for trauma one."

"Sounds like fun."

Kenny chuckled. "You have no idea." He went to his locker and removed his jacket. "See you tomorrow."

"Enjoy your day."

He waved as he left the lounge. She opened her locker and hung her coat and placed her things inside. She removed her stethoscope and wound it around her neck, then put the light blue cap on over her hair. She was ready for the day and whatever it would bring.

As she stepped outside the locker room doors, she was accosted by a paramedic wheeling a man on a gurney into the closest available trauma room. Three hours passed before she had a break. She took a seat next to Janet and put her feet up on the reception desk. "Is your sister still director at that memory care nursing home?"

"Liz?" She nodded. "They've been pretty full for a while. Why? You know someone looking?"

"The mother of a friend has Alzheimer's."

Janet gave a look. "Mrs. Harrison? Things are getting bad with her. I was here both times when they brought her in. And the son, your friend? He's taking a lot of abuse."

"I'm worried about him."

"You should be. He seemed like a man on the edge. I'm just worried about what it might take to push him over."

"Me, too."

Janet took out her phone, pressed a button and handed it to April. "Liz's personal cell. You might want to check with her to see if she has room."

The phone rang and a woman answered. April nodded to Janet, then took the phone to the staff lounge, where it was quieter. She explained Zach's situation and asked Liz if she had space for his mom. "Unfortunately, there's a waiting list. Has your friend consulted a doctor regarding her care?"

"He's relying on a doctor who doesn't seem to be giving him the best advice." She told her about the two emergency room visits. "Her aggression is increasing, and the medication she's been prescribed isn't helping. My friend is getting frustrated."

"Understandable. I do know of a new facility that has space not far from Detroit General. I can give you the number if you'd like. In the meantime, we can set up an appointment for you and your friend to visit us. Get his mom's name on the waiting list."

April took down the information and thanked Liz, promising to have Zach reach out to set up a meeting. She returned to Janet's desk and handed her the phone. "You were right. She doesn't have room, but I have another place Zach can check out for now."

"Will he follow through on it?"

"He will when he's desperate enough."

Janet murmured, "How much worse does it have to get?"

ZACH STARTLED AT the knock on the door. He'd fallen asleep again in the recliner next to his mom's bed. She sat, watching *Judge Judy*. He patted her on the shoulder reassuringly before leaving the bedroom. At the back door was April, a hand on an orange-sherbet-colored bike. It suited her. "Hey."

She dug into her pocket and pulled out a folded piece of paper. "Some names of places and phone numbers for memory care facilities nearby. The top one has a waiting list, but the second one is taking patients."

Oh. He opened the paper and nodded at the information. "Thanks."

"Spaces are limited, so you'll want to check them out soon." She turned and started to straddle her bike.

He stepped forward and put a hand on the handlebars. "Do you have to go?"

"I'm meeting my friends for dinner. Have to get home and change. Page starts chemo tomorrow." She adjusted the helmet on her head. "If you need someone to go with you, let me know and I can check my schedule. Or ask your grandmother. You won't want to go by yourself because it can overwhelm you. It's better to have someone with you."

"Thanks."

She nodded and took a deep breath before boosting herself up onto the seat, but he still had his hand on the handlebars. The bike swayed, and she crashed into him. He caught her in his arms and looked down at her sweet face. Her eyes fluttered closed, and he thought about how nice it would be to be able to kiss her. Instead, he got her back on her feet. "You don't want to be late for your dinner."

She blushed. "Thanks. Good night."

He watched as she coasted down his driveway and turned right to bike to her house two streets over.

Returning to his mom's bedroom, he found the program had ended, and the news had started. He turned the channel to a rerun of an old sitcom since the real world tended to upset his mom. She wrinkled her nose. "I'm bored with television."

Zach cringed, not wanting to hear what she was about to propose. "What would you rather do?"

"I want to go out. Your friend had a bike. Can I get a bike?"

The thought of her trying to ride a bike and getting lost in the neighborhood made him shudder. "Not right now. Are you hungry?"

She looked away from him. "I never get to go anywhere. You lock me inside this house, and I always stay home."

"Do you want to go for a drive?" At least, he could control where she was in that scenario.

"I want to go shopping."

"No."

She pouted. "We never do anything."

"Because you're sick, Mom. I can't take you anywhere without worrying about you getting lost or upset. No, we can either go for a drive, or we can stay here."

"You're so mean."

"I know." He put his hands on his hips. "So what's it going to be?"

"It's getting dark. Your father will be home soon, and he'll take me out somewhere nice." She pointed to her stained top. "I better change." She stood and walked to her closet and opened the door, peering inside at the few things that still hung on hangers. "What happened to my other clothes?"

"You took them out and ripped them."

"I can't go anywhere like this. I need some nice clothes." She chose a white blouse. "Thank goodness this goes with anything. But I don't have a skirt to match. Your father likes it when I show off my legs."

The conversation made him tired and sad. He tried to change its direction. "We have leftover lasagna for dinner."

She returned to her bed and sat on the edge. "He's not coming home, is he?"

"He hasn't for over twenty years, Mom. He's never coming home again." Zach went and put an arm around her shoulders as she started to cry. "But you have me. I won't leave you. Not ever."

She reached up and touched his cheek. "You're a good son."

But he wasn't. Because he was about to break his promise. He fingered the note in his jeans pocket that April had given him. It was time to find a home for his mother, and a good son wouldn't be looking forward to some freedom and peace.

APRIL ENTERED THE pizzeria and scanned the dining room for her friends. Sherri was there, waving. Page must not have arrived yet. April hugged Sherri at the table before removing her jacket and hanging it along with her purse over her chair. "Page is probably running late."

Sherri handed her a menu. "It's her habit."

"I've tried to break her out of it. Even told

her an earlier time to arrive so she'd be on time, but she still shows up late. I don't get it."

Page breezed in the front door and joined them at the table. "I swear, traffic has a vendetta against me. A clear road will suddenly fill with cars when I turn onto it."

"It's not traffic, it's you," April insisted, smiling.

She handed a menu to her friend, but Page waved it away. "I already know what I want. And just to warn you both, there's going to be a lot of food on this table and we're going to enjoy every bite. No worrying about calories or fat content or carbs. I don't know when I'll have an appetite after tonight."

The waitress came, and they deferred to Page's wishes as she ordered two kinds of pizza, wings with blue cheese dressing on the side, garlic bread sticks and, finally, the deluxe salad topped with extra croutons. April smirked at this until Page shrugged. "Gotta have something green."

"The green peppers on the pizza don't count?" April teased.

"I like their salads, so sue me." She gave

the menus to the waitress, who disappeared to put in their order.

Sherri produced a teal gift bag and handed it to Page. "It's not quite what the two of you gave me when I was starting chemo. But I thought you deserved to have some good things while you're going through it."

Page shook her head. "You didn't need to do that, but thank you." She pulled out fuzzy socks, lip balm, hand lotion and peppermint hard candies. "All of these will definitely come in handy."

April passed her a thin gift in black-and-white-decorated paper, tied with a turquoise ribbon. "You can probably guess what this is."

Page unwrapped the journal and sighed. "Really? Writing my thoughts didn't help me get through it the last time."

"Because you didn't actually write any. You carried the journal with you, but I'm betting it's still blank." She opened to the first page, where she'd written her own message to encourage Page. "I started it for you this time."

"Are you going to give me the whole 'chemo is what you make of it' speech?"

Page flipped through the pages of the journal, then placed it on the table between them and grabbed April's hand. "I know what to expect this time. I know that a positive attitude will affect how I handle it, but I don't want to hear your happy, happy mumbo jumbo tonight, okay? Let's just eat and talk about something besides cancer."

April watched Page as Sherri launched into a work story about how she and her new partner with Border Patrol had taken down a computer hacker who had been selling personal credit card information to an international cartel. Page made the appropriate comments and gestures, but April could see she was only going through the motions. She knew her friend well enough to realize that as much as she told them not to talk about cancer, it consumed her thoughts. The waitress started delivering their food, and they filled their plates and chatted while they ate.

When Sherri left the table to go to the restroom, April turned to Page. "What is it you're not saying?" Page drank some of her water instead of answering, so April narrowed her brows at her. "What's going on?"

"It's nothing."

April cocked her head to the side and stared at her friend. "Is it Chad? So help me if that jerk is making things worse for you." Page's ex-husband had the nasty habit of popping back into her life at the worst times. Cancer couldn't be any worse.

"I haven't heard from him in months."

"Your mother?"

"She won't be going with me this round. Told me she's had enough of hospitals to last a lifetime. That if I would accept my mortality, I wouldn't fight against my body so much."

"Nice. But she's not the reason your eyes and nose are red. And don't say it's just allergies."

Page picked slowly at the toppings on her pizza. "I always thought I'd be a mom, and now I'm never going to have a baby. And with my history of cancer, it's not like an adoption agency is going to approve me."

"Didn't you discuss with your doctor about having your eggs frozen beforehand?"

"My ovaries are damaged from the chemotherapy I've already had. Even if I didn't have cancer, it wouldn't be an option. I should have done that three years ago when I first got diagnosed with breast cancer, but I didn't think of it. I didn't know what would happen. And now it's too late."

"Don't say that. If you feel that you're supposed to be a mother, then you will be. Maybe not in the way you expect, but it will happen. I know it."

"I wish I had your faith, but the truth is things like that don't happen to me."

"Don't be such a cynic. That's not going to help you."

Sherri returned to the table, and Page gave a quick shake of her head that tabled the conversation. Page changed topics and asked Sherri about how marriage was treating her.

At the end of the meal, April paid the bill and waved off her friends' offers to help. "My treat. You guys can get the next time."

"Considering that I'll be eating crackers and drinking ginger ale for the next few months, I doubt that I'll be treating anytime soon," Page said.

April put an arm around Page's shoulders.

"You never know. You could breeze through chemo. Third time's the charm, right?"

Page rolled her eyes, but laughed. "We'll see."

CHAPTER ELEVEN

THE ADMINISTRATOR OF the second care facility they visited ushered them to her office. Zach took a seat and Nonna the other. He'd called April to ask her to stay with his mother while they toured the place.

He'd been impressed by the outside of the building as they had walked up to the entrance. It was well kept, bright and cheery, painted in a sunny yellow that reminded him of April's house. Piped-in music played over the speakers in the lobby, a jazzy number that made him want to snap his fingers. Bright colors popped everywhere as they approached the administrator's office, and an aroma of something floral wafted throughout. It was an explosion on his senses.

Zach shifted in the chair, uneasy to be there. Okay, so he reminded himself that he needed to see if this home would be a fit for his mother. Holly Fields, the administrator, cleared her throat and spoke in a kind, but firm manner. "Sunny Meadows is a full-service facility with a special wing for our memory care patients like your mother. We provide treatment for the patient, of course, but also have classes and counseling for family members. We know that placing your parent in a facility is not an easy decision, and we strive to make things easier. To give you peace of mind."

Sounded good so far. He leaned forward in his chair. "My mother has early-onset Alzheimer's. Had it for years, and she's becoming angry and violent. Is your staff equipped to handle her outbursts?"

"We have patients all along the spectrum of dementia, so I can assure you that we understand the different needs of each patient. Those outbursts might be due to a drug reaction or something deeper going on. We have doctors and nurses who can recommend treatment based on your mother's issues." Holly raised an eyebrow, inviting any more questions. She handed a brochure to each of them. "Most of the answers to your questions can be found in here, but I'm more than happy to address them. I've arranged a tour of our facility with my activity coordinator, Mary." Holly gestured to a young woman standing just outside the doorway. "You can explore, then have lunch with some of our residents, if you'd like. We'll end the tour in my office, where we can talk logistics."

Like how much a place like this would cost. Luckily, Zach had been blessed in his career and could afford the best for his mother. He stood and helped his grandmother to her feet. Mary pulled her long black hair over one shoulder as she ushered them out of the office. "I'm the activity coordinator, which means I'm responsible for the social well-being of our patients. I arrange game nights, classes and outings to fulfill the residents' needs for connection. We also encourage our families to join their loved ones in the activities."

She led them through the building, showing them the craft room with cupboards stocked with supplies, the gymnasium and pool, and a room of one of the residents. Zach walked into the patient's room and gaped at the personal items that made the space seem less like a hospital and more like an actual home. He turned to Mary. "Is this a room in the memory care wing?"

Mary shook her head. "The residents on this floor are more independent, but I'd be happy to show you that."

Farther along the hall, Mary pointed out the greenhouse where residents would be soon planting flowers, fruits and vegetables. "We encourage everyone who wants to be involved. Then we use what we grow here at the facility."

She used the name badge hanging from her neck to let them into the next wing. "Our memory care residents require more security for their safety, so we have them in a wing that is constantly monitored." A patient's door was open and Mary knocked. The older woman sitting in a rocking chair working with a crochet hook and yarn smiled. "Good morning, Margaret. How is that baby blanket coming?"

The older woman tittered and held up the bright pink item. It looked like the beginning of a square. "Eleven granny squares down and only fourteen more to go."

"That's great. Do you mind if our guests take a look at your room?"

The older woman quit crocheting and swept an arm grandly. "Help yourself."

Nonna entered first, and Zach went next, surveying the personal touches, but also noticing the medical equipment, including the hospital bed. But still, the room felt cozier than he had expected.

Margaret held up the crocheted square to him. "Do you see any mistakes?"

He wouldn't know one if he did see one. "Nope."

"Ha! That's because there aren't any. I'm the expert. Not like Phyllis, who thinks she knows better than I do." The tip of her tongue tucked in the corner of her mouth, she returned to her blanket.

Mary had them check out two more resident rooms before she showed them to the dining room. "Lunch will be starting in a few minutes if you'd like to stay and eat with some of the residents."

Zach shook his head, but Nonna paused. "I'd like to talk to some of them, if we could. You don't mind, do you?"

"You go ahead. I'll head back to the office and discuss details with the director."

He waited until Nonna took a seat at one of the tables with a number of the residents before leaving. As he strode down the hall, he used the time to remove his personal feelings and focus instead on the business at hand. The facility looked bright and clean. The staff seemed confident, though he hadn't seen any giving care to determine if they were competent. The residents appeared to be happy and relaxed. He'd already called around and gotten recommendations from others who had placed their parents or relatives in homes. Sunny Meadows came highly praised.

He knocked on the administrator's door and popped his head inside. "I hope I'm not interrupting, but I'm ready to talk through those logistics."

Holly stood and indicated a chair with her hand. "Absolutely, Mr. Harrison. I'm here to deal with any questions or concerns you might have."

For the next half hour, he quizzed her, and she patiently answered everything and a few more questions he hadn't thought to ask. They discussed payment options that would work for his budget and timetables for placement. She gave him a list of doctors who were on staff and more who consulted on a regular basis. She handed him testimonials of patients and families. His unease at the beginning of the day subsided until he felt an inevitability. This was a place he could see his mother living in. One that might help her to thrive rather than deteriorate the way she was at home. She'd be surrounded by people even when he had to work late. She'd have access to immediate medical care.

And he'd be able to sleep at night knowing that she would be safe and sound.

"I'd like to discuss this with my grandmother, but I'm impressed by what I've seen."

"I know you're worried about your mother. We will do our best to make her feel comfortable here. We could have a room available by the end of the week, if you need it."

Three days? It felt too soon. Too early to be talking about moving her in, right? He stood and shook her hand, then he found Nonna, still in the dining room, laughing at something one of the residents shared.

She seemed to fit right in with them, and he hoped his mother would, too.

APRIL HELPED MRS. HARRISON put her head over the kitchen sink as she rinsed the shampoo with the handheld nozzle. "You're going to feel so much better with clean hair."

The soap away, April wrapped a towel around the older woman's wet head and helped her straighten up. Once Mrs. Harrison was settled in a dining room chair, April combed her hair, working at any snarls. "How does that feel, Mrs. Harrison?"

Kate's eyes closed as the comb moved through her hair. "Wonderful, dear. But you should call me Kate, that's my name. Zach tries with my hair, but he isn't nearly as good as you are." She reached up and touched a strand. "You really should be a hairdresser. You have magic hands."

"I hope my patients think the same thing."

Her hair cleaned and detangled, Kate motioned for April to take a seat next to her. "Now, tell me about you and my son." She wagged a finger at her when April started to protest. "I've seen how you look at each other. I may not remember a lot of things, but I know what it's like to look at the man I love."

"Were you and Robert happy?"

"We are, even though he's not around as much as I'd like. I keep waiting for him to walk through that door with roses and a smile that's meant only for me." She glanced at the front door and sighed. "I can't remember the last time I saw him."

"You loved him very much."

Kate nodded. "And don't think I didn't notice how you sidestepped my question about Zach. Do you love him?"

"I don't know. We haven't had much time to figure that out."

"Because of me."

"Because of our careers. And friends. And all the busyness of life that gets in the way of getting to know someone."

"There is a lot of noise in this world, but if it matters to you both, then you'll find a quiet space to find each other."

April smiled and patted Kate's hand. "You're one smart cookie, Mrs. Harrison. Kate."

"Do we have cookies?" She pointed toward the kitchen, her eyes bright and her face fading into a childlike pose. "I love the ones with the frosting in the middle. My madre goes to the bakery to buy the Italian ones, but they're not the same."

April stood and walked to the kitchen. When she returned with the cookies, April realized Kate had retreated into an earlier memory as she softly hummed a nursery rhyme. She took the cookies that April handed her and nibbled at them.

A pang hit April in her chest. For a few moments, it had been nice to see the Kate who could have been had her disease not taken her away. She choked back the tears and marveled that Zach had lived with this for so long. She leaned over and kissed the top of Kate's head.

The back door opened, and Zach entered. He shook off the rain from his jacket and hung it on a hook before joining them in the dining room. "Am I in time for cookies?"

Kate held up her half-eaten crescent. "They're just like the ones Madre brings home from the store."

"Because that's where they still come from." He put an arm around her shoulders. "And April washed your hair, too."

"Your father will be pleased to see me looking so nice when he gets home from work."

Zach nodded and motioned with his head for April to join him in the kitchen. He poured two glasses of milk and offered her one. She waved it away. "How did the tours go?"

"We really liked the second one, Sunny Meadows. Although the last one was great, it's got a waiting list that means she wouldn't be able to get in until next year if we're lucky. And she doesn't have the luxury of time."

He took his mother one of the glasses of milk and came back to have a sip of his own, leaving a faint mustache. April smirked and handed him a napkin. He thanked her and glanced out toward his mom. "How was she?"

"We had a great conversation for a little while, then she was gone."

"That sounds about right. I can't predict how long those moments will last, or if they'll show up at all."

"What are you going to do?"

"Move her to Sunny Meadows. I think she'll be happy there."

"And you?"

He shrugged and finished his milk, putting his empty glass in the sink. "My feelings don't count in all of this. What matters is what's best for her. That used to be me, but she needs more than that now."

April reached for his hand. "I'd be happy to help you with the move if I can."

He cleared his throat and looked over at her. "I wouldn't be able to do it without you." He gave her a quick hug, then left the kitchen to join his mother at the dining room table. "Mom, I've got some good news."

THE MOVE TOOK place the following Saturday morning. He'd talked about Sunny Meadows with his mom every day so that she wouldn't be surprised by all the activity. Still, when the morning arrived, he had to remind her three times that she was leaving. "Why? I promise I'll be good."

"They can take better care of you than I can."

"But I want to stay with you. Are you moving with me?"

"No, just you. You'll have your own room."

"I have my own room here."

"The nurses and doctors will be able to look after you."

"But you look after me."

He fought for patience. Every argument he had, she would have one to counter. "Mom, we've talked about this. I can't keep you safe and healthy, but they can. I'll be there to visit you as much as I can."

She pouted and shook her head. "No. I'm not going."

"Yes, you are. April is coming over very soon. You remember April? She's going to give us a hand to get you into your new room." He hoped that the novelty of April would ease her worries and nerves. He could see the signs of another fit starting to form behind the stubborn expression on her face. "She's so excited about this new place."

"Is she moving there, too?"

"No, Mom, just you."

"I don't want to go, and you can't make me."

That's where she was wrong. He could and

would make her move into the facility. This day was hard enough, but the pushback that he received from her compounded his guilt, but confirmed he was doing the right thing. "Did you pack your book? You don't want to forget it here." He heard a knock on the back door. "That's probably April. Find your book while I let her in, okay?"

She searched her room, and he left to go answer the door. He found April standing in the drizzling rain. "I put my bike in your garage. I hope you don't mind."

"You're really getting around on that thing."

"It was on my second-chance list. I'm preparing for a bike tour of Detroit that's coming up." She stepped past him, and he could smell the rain and a scent of oranges that was all April. "Are you ready for today?"

He grinned as he closed the back door and followed April up the three stairs to the kitchen. She went directly to his mother's room. "Hey, Kate. Big day today, huh? Are you excited?"

"Tell him he can't make me do it. I want to stay here." His mom tugged on April's sleeve.

"Tell him I can stay. I promise to be good and eat all my vegetables."

April glanced back at him and put an arm around his mom. "But imagine all the new friends you're going to have. They even have better cooks than Zach. And they have a room full of games and puzzles, and another with crafts. Doesn't that sound like fun?"

"Maybe." His mom put a hand over April's.

"That's it, Kate. Do you have everything? Did you remember your book?"

His mother clutched it to her chest. "Can we read it now?"

"How about we read it once we get to your new room?"

She gave a nod and let April put it in the suitcase that lay open on her bed. "Anything else you want to take? Do you have something that's your favorite?"

"Zach said I can take my TV."

Zach stepped forward. "I already packed it in the car for you."

His mother took a quick survey of the room. "I think I have it all."

"If you forget anything, I can bring it tomorrow when I visit," he said and zipped up the suitcase, then hefted it off the bed. "Should we go?"

April helped his mom into a jacket with a hood. "It's raining out, and we don't want you to get wet." She led his mom out first, and he followed with the suitcase.

April sat in the back seat of the car with his mother. "She'll feel more comfortable that way," she told him.

During the drive, April chatted about the weather and her hopes that the incessant rain would mean more flowers in time for Easter. Zach appreciated how she distracted not only his mother with her nonstop talk, but him, as well. He'd woken up with a headache, and arguing with his mother about the move hadn't helped it any. Having April there gave him a buffer with his mother and his own emotions.

As they got closer to the nursing home, his headache migrated to his belly and seemed to squeeze him in the gut. He pulled into a parking spot and took a deep breath before getting out of the car and opening the door for his mom. She looked up at the building and wrinkled her nose. "It's yellow."

April linked her arm through hers. "It reminds me of my house. It's bright and sunny and makes me happy."

"It is pretty," his mom agreed.

"There you go."

April gave him a grin, took the handle of the rolling suitcase with her free hand, and helped his mom walk up to the entrance. Zach followed with the television set. They met Holly in the lobby. Zach had stopped by the day before to sign the paperwork and make the first payment for his mother's new room. Holly had assured him that he was doing the responsible thing, but the farther they walked through the building, the more doubts assailed him. Was this really the best choice? Would she be happy there? How would her life, and his, change with this move?

Holly saw them through the doors to the secure wing and to a room near the end of the hall. The administrator opened the door where a sign welcomed his mom to her new home. His mother hesitated.

"Don't you want to see it?" April asked as his mom hesitated for a moment.

His mother looked back at him, and the doubts he felt were reflected on her face. He wanted to say, "I agree. This is too much, too soon. Let's go home and we'll both be good." But he didn't. He swallowed his fear and guilt. "Look. They made you a sign for your new room. It has your name and rainbows, your favorite."

He released a pent-up breath when his mother nodded and stepped forward. He followed her inside, placing the television set on a dresser that came with the room. He glanced at April. "I'll go and get the other things."

She put a hand on his arm. "It's going to be okay."

He put a hand over hers for a second or two before he nodded and left the room. Holly accompanied him to the lobby. "When you want to enter the memory care wing, remember to press the blue button on the door for the nurse to buzz you in."

He got to his car and opened the trunk. He'd bought new sheets and a comforter set for the occasion. Probably should have washed them before bringing them over, he thought, but time had gotten away from him, and now it was too late. He put his hand on the trunk to close it, but he paused and allowed himself to let the guilt and fear in for a moment. Pushing those thoughts away, he slammed the trunk shut, feeling as though he was also shutting the door on his guilt and worry. He had to keep a happy face on for his mother. Had to show her that everything was going to be all right even if he had his doubts.

When he returned to the room, April was unpacking the suitcase while his mother chatted with another resident. His mom looked up and smiled at him. "This is Margery, who lives three doors down. She loves *Judge Judy* almost as much as I do."

"That's good, Mom." He opened the bag with the sheets and removed the plastic that covered them and started to make the bed.

"That's my son, Zach. He's always good to me."

"My son, Ben, visits every Sunday afternoon, so you'll have to meet him next time he comes." Margery put a hand on the bright blue sheets. "What a pretty color."

"It's my favorite."

"Mine, too!"

The two women continued to get to know

each other as April and Zach put the room together. With her clothes arranged in the dresser and her bed made up in the new linens, the room started to take on his mother's personality. He figured they could take her to lunch and go buy some plants that would brighten up the space even more. At this point, she could request an entire flower shop, and he'd agree and pull out his credit card.

After lunch and picking up some last-minute things, they walked his mother to her room. She'd asked at lunch if he could bring over the recliner so she could sit by the window and look out into the gardens. He'd assured her that he'd hire someone to transport it to the nursing home. She sat on the bed and picked up the book, holding it out to him. "One more chapter?"

He nodded and took a seat next to her on the bed. He found the place they'd left off the last time and started to read. She rested her head on his shoulder, and he breathed in the floral scent of her shampoo, storing this memory away to pull out when he missed her. April leaned against the far wall and listened as he read.

The chapter over, he handed his mother the book. "We can read the next chapter tomorrow when I visit."

"Promise?"

He did so and kissed her forehead. "April and I have to go now. Do you need anything else?"

His mother looked around the room and frowned. "I wish you didn't have to go so soon."

"I know, Mom." Truth was, the longer he stretched out the visit, the harder it got to get up and leave. He had to do it. To walk out of the facility and leave her behind. And he'd found excuses to put it off until he didn't have any more. "I'll be back tomorrow afternoon for lunch."

She turned to April. "You, too?"

"I'd love to, Kate, but I have plans already. I will visit soon, though." She walked over to Zach and took his hand in hers. "We need to leave."

Zach kissed his mom again, then stood and followed April to the door. He turned and fought the tears that threatened at the back of his throat. "Love you, Mom."

"You, too, Zach. You'll tell your father where to find me?"

"You know I will."

All the way down the hall, April squeezed his hand. "Stay strong for just a little longer. Wait until we get out into the parking lot."

He nodded and kept facing forward. They moved briskly through the lobby. He waved at Holly before walking out the front doors and down the sidewalk that led to the parking lot. When they reached his car, he pulled April into his arms and buried his face into her shoulder.

She held him as he cried, rubbing his back and whispering words of comfort. He clung to her and kept his eyes shut, letting the fear and doubt fill his body and empty into his tears. April put a hand on the back of his head and stroked his hair. "She'll be okay, Zach. This is the best place for her."

"I know."

"You don't have to worry. They'll take good care of her."

"I know. So why am I so upset?"

"Because you've been taking care of her on your own since you were a kid, and it's hard to let someone else take over." April cupped his face in her hands so that he had to look down at her, and he saw tears on her cheeks, too.

He stared into her baby blue eyes and found a safe place for him to fall. "You've been amazing through all this. I don't think I could have survived today on my own. Thank you for being here."

"It's been my honor."

He took a deep shuddering breath, and she wiped his tears away with her thumbs. They shared a smile, tremulous at best, then got into the car. They held hands as he drove out of the parking lot and back to his empty house.

He turned to her and smiled. "Would you like to go out tomorrow night? Just the two of us for dinner."

"You don't need to repay me."

"No, I was thinking more like a date. Our third, if my math is correct."

She blushed and dipped her head. "Yes. I'd love to."

CHAPTER TWELVE

APRIL PROPPED HER bike next to the porch, jogged up the steps to the door and knocked. Waiting, she looked out at the street and other houses. It was barely spring, and most of the snow had melted in preparation for the changing season. She couldn't wait until the warmer air became scented with lilacs and tulips. She twitched her nose in anticipation and smiled. The front door opened, and Page glared out at her. "What?"

"Is that any way to greet your best friend who brought you treats?" She held up the plastic bag that had ginger ale and saltine crackers. "They're your favorite."

"Hardly." Page stepped aside and waved her inside. "I'm going to go collapse on the sofa, if you don't mind."

"I volunteered to come and stay with you on your bad days, you know." She put the plastic bag on the coffee table, pulled a crocheted afghan from the back of the sofa and covered Page with it. "It's pretty bad this time, huh?"

Page moaned and tugged the blanket over her head. "Please stop talking. Everything hurts. I'm nauseous. And all I want to do is sleep."

"Do you need anything?"

"No. Sherri stopped over earlier with groceries, and Mom called with a pep talk."

April rolled her eyes. She knew Mrs. Kosinski's idea of encouraging Page. It usually started with a list of things she'd done to cause the trouble herself and concluded with a guilt trip about her not visiting often enough. "Then you definitely needed me to come over." She took a seat in the recliner next to the sofa where Page lay. "Are you taking leave from work?"

"No, but I'm going down to part-time hours. I don't need extra time at home to feel sorry for myself, but I can't put in full days like I have been." She tucked the afghan under her chin. "Luckily, Joanne didn't want to lose me, so she agreed to my demands."

April shook her head, but smiled. "Your

supervisor would do whatever you asked because she knows you're the best."

"I'm not sure. There's a new girl who started that could be a threat to my status as favorite."

April reached over and touched her hand. "You're always my favorite."

"You're easy to please." But Page grinned at this. "So how did the big move go?"

"He's emotional, which is understandable. I mean, he's been taking care of her for so long. I'm afraid that he'll feel a little lost without the day-to-day responsibility weighing him down." She shrugged and glanced at her hands. "He did ask me out for dinner tonight, though."

Page's mouth formed an O, and she chuckled. "Well, well, well. Looks like he's making his move."

"According to him, it will be our third date."

"So it's getting serious."

April wasn't convinced. Sure, they'd shared some meals together. She'd helped him as he settled his mother in the new facility. He'd even treated her to upgrades to her New York

City visit. But serious? It seemed like they should have had a conversation about that. Maybe that was what the dinner invitation was about. He wanted to talk about them as a couple.

Page turned onto her side and moaned as she moved. "I hate this part of treatment."

"I didn't know you had a part you enjoyed."

"I like it when it's over." She adjusted her blanket. "Dr. Frazier's talking about three months on chemo, then a month off, surgery, and another three months depending on my numbers."

"So we'll hope that you won't need any more after surgery."

Page laughed, but she didn't sound amused. "You know my history. I have bad luck when it comes to cancer."

"Luck or not, you can beat this. And I'll be here every step of the way."

"That's what I'm worried about."

April rolled her eyes a second time, but chuckled. "You love me, and you know it. You couldn't get through this without me."

"That's because you won't let me try it on my own."

The two friends grinned at each other. Finally, Page closed her eyes. "I hope you won't think I'm a bad friend if I take a nap. I don't think I can keep my eyes open any longer."

"You sleep. I'll clean."

Page's eyes flew open, and she propped herself up on one elbow. "You don't have to do that."

"It's not like you're going to feel up to doing it for a while." She pressed at Page to lie back down on the sofa. "I won't mess up how you keep things. I know what a neat freak you are."

"No switching cans around in the cupboard, or hanging my clothes up out of order?"

April knew that Page liked stuff organized alphabetically or by color. It was probably a reaction to the chaos that she'd grown up with in her mother's house. "Don't worry. I'll put everything where it belongs."

"I've got shelves labeled if you get confused."

"Of course you do." April felt her friend's forehead with the back of her hand and frowned. "You seem a little warm. I'll bring you an aspirin if you think you can keep it down."

"It's probably a side effect, but I'll keep an eye on it."

"So will I." She retrieved the bottle of aspirin and brought it to Page. She shook two pills into Page's hand and watched as her friend swallowed the medication with water. "Get some sleep. You can't risk getting sick on top of everything else."

"Yes, Doctor."

APRIL SAT AT a table and played with the paper from her straw, winding it around her fingers one way, then rewinding it the other way. She glanced at her watch. Zach had said he'd meet her at the popular barbecue place after his visit with his mom, but he was almost an hour late. The waiter stopped by the table and pointed to the other chair. She shook her head. "He hasn't arrived yet, but I'm sure he'll be here soon."

She took out her cell phone and shot off a quick text asking where he was. She glanced around the crowded restaurant and watched several happy couples as they chatted over their meals. Sighing, she looked at the empty chair. Checked her phone. Still no response.

The front door opened and Zach breezed in. He smiled when he spotted her. "Sorry. She didn't want me to leave tonight," he said as he collapsed into a chair.

April accepted his excuse. "It's fine. She's still nervous about being in a new place without you. She'll adjust."

"I'm meeting with the medical staff Wednesday night so that we can discuss her treatment plan. In the meantime, they're running tests and adjusting her medication."

"Good. She needed that." April handed him a menu. "I'm starving."

"Me, too. I was there most of the day and didn't get a chance to eat." He perused the choices.

April set her menu down. "Even though she's not in the house with you, you still need to take care of yourself. How did you sleep?"

"Sleep? What's that?" When she gave him a look, he laughed and shook his head. "I got a full eight hours. Even if I did wake up a couple of times thinking that I heard her calling for me."

"I'm serious. You can't keep going like you are or you'll end up in my ER with exhaustion."

"I'm fine."

The waiter arrived and they ordered their meals. April sat back in her seat, not ready to let it go. "Are you sure?"

"Well, it's not the same without her there."

"This is an adjustment for you both."

He reached across the table and took her hand in his. "I don't want to talk about my mom anymore. I'd rather talk about us." He kissed one of her knuckles. "I have more freedom in my life, and I'd like to explore it with you."

Her chest got warm and her breath caught in her throat. "Really?"

He smiled at the crack in her voice. "Yes. I want to help you with your list. What do you have planned next?"

The list? Why couldn't she think rationally when he looked at her in that way? She scrambled for a coherent idea. "A bike tour of an older neighborhood in Detroit. It's this coming Saturday. Would you like to come with me?"

"Bike tour, huh?" He rubbed the back of his neck, and she wasn't sure if he was interested in it or not. "I haven't been on a bike in years."

"Neither was I until a few weeks ago."

He gave a nod. "All right, I'll do it. Do you want me to pick you up?"

"Actually, I'll give you the directions to where we have to meet. I was planning on riding my bike there instead of driving."

"Oh. Okay."

"And my one year anniversary of being cancer-free is coming up, so I'm throwing a party."

"I'll definitely be there for that. I'll even bring chips."

Their salads came, and Zach dug into his. She paused and watched him as he shoveled the lettuce into his mouth. "You must be really hungry."

He stopped the fork midway to his mouth. "I am. Like I said before, I didn't want to leave my mom, so I skipped lunch." He finished his bite, then wiped his mouth with a napkin. "I got good news. I called my boss, and I return to work on Tuesday."

"That's great. I'm sure you're anxious to get back to a normal routine."

"My normal involved worrying about my mother's mental state, and if I was going to get called out of an important meeting to go take care of something she needed." He lowered his head to stare at the plate and picked at the salad. "What I'm living now is something completely different."

Now it was her turn to reach over and grab his hand. "I know that you're confused and hurting, but it's going to be okay. You'll find you will be happier in the long run."

He raised his head to glare at her. "How can I be happy when my mother is wondering where I am? She thinks I'm leaving her in there and will never visit."

"You know that you're going to be there checking up on her as much as you can."

"But she doesn't believe that."

"You both need to adjust to this new reality. Everything will be okay."

He removed his hand from hers and put it in his lap. "Right now, I don't need these platitudes. Let me have my feelings. I'm angry and concerned."

April bit her lip to keep from saying anything and forked a piece of lettuce instead. Zach sipped his water, looking everywhere in the room but at her. They ate in silence until the server arrived to remove their half-eaten salads. "Zach, I'm not saying that you can't be hurt or upset. I'm saying that eventually you'll both be better off."

He stood and removed some bills from his wallet and threw them on the table. "I apologize for my bad mood, but I can't sit here right now. Maybe dinner tonight was a bad idea. I'll talk to you later."

April watched openmouthed as he left the restaurant without her.

ZACH SAT IN his car for a few moments, stewing in his thoughts. He hadn't meant to get so mad at April. He'd come this evening hoping to start a real relationship with her, to talk about a future together. But her optimism had grated against his sour mood. It wasn't her fault that he'd left his mother's room at the nursing home wondering if he'd done the right thing. She didn't know that his mother's tears as he left had fed the guilt that already filled his chest.

He knew in his brain that moving his mother to the nursing home was best for both of them, but his heart ached with how miserable she seemed each time he left. Maybe April was right. It would get easier with time, but for now it bothered him and left him feeling like a terrible son.

He started his car and glanced out the windshield. April stood under the front awning of the restaurant, two plastic food containers in her hands. Her shoulders hunched over, she walked in the opposite direction. He debated for a few seconds, then opened his car door and called her name. She paused and turned at the sound, but stood on the sidewalk staring at him. He crossed the street to reach her, not looking to see if oncoming traffic headed his way. A car blared its horn at him, but he didn't care.

As he approached her, she didn't smile or give him any encouragement. But then he'd acted enough of a jerk earlier that he had to be the one to make the first move. He put his hands on both sides of her face and peered into her eyes. "Forgive me? You've done nothing but be supportive and sweet, and I'm sorry for taking my anger out on you."

She blinked a few times, then nodded. "I only want what's best for you. You have to believe that."

"I do. And that's what makes you so special." He placed a soft kiss on her mouth, and she leaned into him when he started to step away. Not wanting to disappoint her, he deepened the kiss. Hoped that he could express with the kiss what he hadn't with his words.

After they broke apart, he wiped the moisture from under her eyes with his thumbs. "Why don't we take the food back to my house? I really need a friend to talk to right now."

She smiled. "I'd like that." She waved at the row of bicycles chained to a black metal rack. "If you take these containers, I'll ride my bike and meet you there."

"Let's put your bike in the back of my car and ride together."

She carried the food while he wheeled the bike to his car. Once the bike was secure, they got in the car and he drove them to his house. They ate right out of the containers in the living room, knee to knee on the sofa. He shared his fears about his mother's condition worsening. She told him about Page's rough reaction to chemo. They finished eating and held hands while they disclosed the things closest to their hearts.

She yawned and glanced at her watch, then bolted upright. "It's after midnight. I have to work tomorrow at six."

He hated to see her go, didn't want to be left alone, but knew she needed to get home. He walked her to the side door and held it open for her. She paused for a moment, then reached up on tiptoe to kiss his cheek. "Good night."

"Wait."

He grabbed her arm and pulled her to him. He lowered his head and touched his lips to hers. She sighed into the kiss.

When they broke apart, she looked as dazed as he felt. He kissed the tip of her nose. "I'll drive you home."

"But my bike…"

"Is already in the back of my car."

THE OFFICE CHATTER quieted as Zach stepped off the elevator and made his way between the rows of cubicles to his office. Dalvin stood as he passed by and followed him inside, closing the door behind him. "That was a fantastic entrance. They'll be talking about it for days among the assistants."

"All I did was walk into my office."

"With your head up and shoulders back. You looked like a conquering warrior returning home from the battle." Dalvin grinned and clapped his hands. "Leslie will be eating her words. She's been saying a lot about you while you were gone."

That was one thing he hadn't missed about being away from the office. Work gossip tended to sour his stomach, and he usually left the room when it started. He placed his messenger bag on his desk and began to remove his laptop and check his phone. "Any updates that I need to know?"

"I've been calling your clients to make sure they're aware that you're back. You'll want to check in with Ramos and Jackson."

"I already called them both this morning. Can you put Jackson's follow-up with his doctor on my appointment calendar for Thursday afternoon?" He plugged his computer in and started it up. "Ramos is in Phoenix for spring training. Get me the number of the place he's staying. I'd like to send him a gift to welcome him to the majors."

Dalvin typed the information into his cell phone. He sighed and walked around the desk to give Zach a hug. "I'm so glad you're back. How's your mom?"

Zach patted Dalvin's back. "She's going to be okay. I'll need to leave early tomorrow afternoon to meet with her doctors. I already told Mike about it."

Dalvin stepped back and typed that into his cell phone. "I'll update your schedule and send it to your computer and phone." He paused and smiled. "We're all pulling for your mom."

"Thanks."

Dalvin left the office, and Zach turned to his computer to work through his email. By the time he'd returned the calls and messages during his absence, his stomach grumbled, telling him it was time for a break. He saved an early draft of a document he'd been reviewing and looked up to find Mike standing in his doorway. "Have lunch plans, Zach?"

"Um…"

"Good. We can go to this sports bar down the street. My treat."

Zach knew better than to refuse, so he grabbed his cell phone and shrugged into his sports coat. They walked the few blocks rather than taking a car since parking was at a premium. It was dark inside the pub, and televisions around the room blared different sports channels. They took a seat at an empty high-top table. Mike looked around and waved at a man in a corner booth. "Be right back. I see a buddy of mine."

A server came, and Zach ordered them glasses of ice water and a basket of bacon and cheese fries to share, knowing how much his boss enjoyed anything fried covered in more fat. Mike returned to the table and drank half the water in his glass. "Zach, you know how much I admire you."

This didn't sound like the start of a good conversation. "Sir, are you firing me?"

"What? No." Mike loosened his tie and peered at Zach. "I know that the decision to put your mom into a nursing home wasn't an easy one. But you did what you had to. It was the smart move…a necessary one."

He shifted uneasily in his seat, not feeling as if he warranted such admiration. "Thank you, sir. I think."

"That's not why I asked you to lunch, though."

The server came with the basket of fries, and they ordered lunch while Zach tried to figure out his boss's agenda. He wasn't getting fired, so why would it be important for them to meet outside of the office? What was he about to say that couldn't be said there?

Mike took a few fries and stuffed them into his mouth. "Speaking of tough decisions being made lately, I wanted you to be the first to know. I'm selling the agency."

Zach frowned, a French fry paused in midair. "I'm sorry, did you say you're quitting?"

"More like retirement. I've been in this business long enough to know that I've lost my killer instinct. Our agency isn't as competitive as it used to be. Sure, you and Leslie are my go-getters, but I'm tired. I'm old. And the wife wants to spend half the year in Florida when the snow flies." Mike gave him a shrug. "We're on top, so why not go out that way?"

"But what about the agents? And all the assistants? What about our clientele?"

"Like I said, I'm interested in selling the agency and all of its assets. Are you interested in buying?"

Zach choked. "Why me?"

"You have a proven track record. Sure, the last few months were patchy, but you've got that solved now. You're free and independent. And I know how well I pay you. You could do this in your sleep."

Zach put down the fry and tried to comprehend what he was being offered. He'd played with the idea of someday owning his own agency, but that was much farther down the road. He was barely thirty. He didn't have the experience yet to be able to lead, did he? "I don't know, Mike. This is coming out of nowhere. I'm just coming off a suspension because I couldn't handle both my personal life and my clients' business."

"But you've solved that now."

"Not quite."

"What is it that's stopping you from taking me up on my once-in-a-lifetime offer? Is it the money? Because we can work out a buyout deal. Is it Leslie? She can handle it. What's keeping you back? Tell me."

"I don't know if I can manage an agency and my own roster of clients. I'm already stretched further beyond what I'm comfortable with."

"So you slowly move your clients to another agent. I had to stop being an agent after a while when I started the company." He gave a shrug as if it didn't matter. "You get to be your own boss and do your own thing."

It was too much to think about at the moment. His worries about his mother were uppermost in his mind, so anything else still came second. And then there was April. He wanted to pursue something with her, but he'd have to focus on the business if he bought the agency from Mike. On the other hand, being the boss sounded nice. He could lead the agency in the direction he wanted. Could fashion the office to reflect what he believed in, focusing on integrity and honesty rather than just the money. He could make his own name in this business.

"It's tempting, Mike. But I'll have to pass."

"Great. I'll have my lawyer draft the paperwork."

Zach frowned at his boss's satisfied smile. "I'm turning you down, Mike. I can't even consider this properly right now. You know what's going on in my life. It's too much."

Mike nodded. "I can wait. By September, you'll be begging to buy it from me."

Zach wasn't sure that he would be. His mom was still his priority. Then clients. Then the agency. And, he hoped, he'd be able to find a place for April in there, too.

SATURDAY MORNING STARTED out cloudy with a forecast of rain. April sipped her coffee as she stood at the kitchen sink, looking out into the backyard at the grass that had started to spring up from the winter-ravaged ground. She hoped that the rain would hold off until after the bike tour. She'd take her raincoat with her, just in case.

When she'd been sick and going through treatment, she'd never expected to be here at this moment in her life. Part of her had wondered if she'd survive. Another, stronger part pushed her to endure and come out stronger. Most days, she felt blessed that she'd gotten to enjoy her life. That was the point of the second-chance list. To savor times like this, a crisp morning, relishing a cup of coffee and the contentment that warmed her from the inside out.

She checked the clock on the microwave, then finished her coffee in one gulp. Didn't want to be late for the beginning of the tour. They kept to a strict timetable that she'd been told about when she'd signed up herself and Zach. The group would leave if you didn't show up by ten.

She put her cornflower blue rain slicker on over her lemon yellow T-shirt and jeans. Tucked her cell phone in one of her front jeans pockets, her ID and some money in the other. Scrutinized her reflection in the mirror one last time, tried to smooth down some of the flyaway curls, but then gave up and left the house.

She retrieved her bike from her garage and walked it to the end of the driveway. Kicking off, she rode past the hospital and toward the park where the tour was to begin. She breathed deeply, enjoying the earthy scent that signaled spring was on its way. Soon, the tulips, lilies and daffodils would push through the dirt and bloom. To April, those flowers represented a beginning more than any others. They heralded the start of friendlier temperatures and more time spent outdoors. Of longer, brighter days. A chance to start again.

The group at the park gathered near the swing set that currently had no swings. Once the weather improved and kids started to fill the park, the city employees would hang the swings back up. For now, the space looked barren. She nodded to several people and checked in with the woman holding a clipboard. "I'm April Sprader. I don't see my friend Zach just yet."

The organizer looked at her watch. "He's got six minutes."

April nodded and returned to her bike. She took out her phone, certain there'd be a message from Zach. Nothing. She sent off a quick text to Page, asking her how she was feeling.

The response came immediately. Fine. Leave me alone. Aren't you supposed to be touring?

Waiting for Zach. It's a beautiful day.

I'll watch it from the window.

A car pulled up in the parking lot and April hoped it was Zach. A family with kids got out instead and joined the group with their bicycles. April turned back to her phone. You on your way? Not that he would stand her up, but he wasn't known for being prompt the few times they'd gone out. And she'd texted him the directions and start time last night. The tour leaves in three minutes.

She waited but didn't get a response. He had to be riding his bike to the park and couldn't reply.

The three minutes passed and April approached the tour guide. "My friend isn't here yet. Is there any way we could wait a few more minutes? He might be stuck in traffic."

"We don't wait for anyone."

April glanced around the park but didn't

see him. "What's your first stop? Maybe we could catch up with you."

The tour guide gave her a list of places they'd be seeing. "And we don't give refunds."

April nodded and stepped back as the organizer called the group together and gave the agenda for the tour. She listened as best she could, but was really straining to hear Zach's car or bike, and missed most of what she said. Zach had to be on his way. Maybe he wasn't sure where the park was. She got out her phone and sent him a quick message. The tour is leaving. Are you close?

Again, no response. The tour group left, some of them waving to April. She propped her bike against a tree and took a seat on the bench of a picnic table. She checked her voice mail to see if he'd called her. Read through her email. Even logged on to Facebook to see if there were any messages from him saying he would be late.

It started to rain about fifteen minutes after the tour group had left. More like a sprinkle or fine mist rather than large raindrops. Still, it was enough for April to pull up her hood and lean over the table in an attempt to stay dry. She wiped the moisture off the screen of her cell phone and dialed Zach's phone number. The call went straight to voice mail. She took a deep breath. "Hey, Zach. It's me, April. We were supposed to meet about twenty minutes ago for the tour. I'm still waiting for you at the park. Please call me so I know that you're okay. Talk to you soon."

She called Page's number. "What?"

"Do you always have to answer your phone that way?"

"It's easier. What do you want? I thought you were on that bike tour thing."

April frowned and scanned the empty park. "Zach hasn't shown up yet, and I'm sitting alone in the park, and it's raining. How long am I required to stay here before I give up on him?"

"He stood you up?"

"No, he's running late. He's like someone else I know."

"I'm not always late. You're just always early."

April smiled at this. "You don't think he's changed his mind about me, do you?"

"Not possible. Something probably came

up. Give him another ten minutes. Though you might want to wait somewhere that's dry."

April ended the call and stood. The trees hadn't started to leaf yet, so huddling under one of them wouldn't give her much protection. The rain had started to fall harder with bigger drops. She peered up at the sky, feeling the water drip down her face and into the crook of her neck. If she didn't find somewhere that had a roof or at least some kind of covering, she risked hypothermia.

The park had a restroom with an eave that jutted over the cement sidewalk. It was better than nothing. She sprinted to it and shivered underneath it. She still had a good view of the parking lot in case he showed. He had to show. He wouldn't stand her up and make her wait in the rain for nothing. Page was right. Something had come up.

The longer she waited, the colder she got. She tried calling and texting him, but didn't hear a word. Forty minutes after the tour group had left, she walked to her bike and straddled it. She could wait at home for him to call.

Riding her bike in the rain wasn't as much fun. She reached her house and dumped the bike in the garage, then ran from it to the front door. She hung up her drenched raincoat and rushed to the bathroom, where she grabbed a towel to dry her hair. The rain slicker had kept her clothes dry at least. Well, mostly dry.

In the living room, she glanced at her phone again. No calls. No texts. Nothing from Zach. This was her last Saturday off before the shift change at the hospital, and she wanted to enjoy it. She was done with waiting. She'd make her own plans.

THE PLANE TOUCHED down in Phoenix with a bump, and Zach's heart restarted as they taxied to the terminal. He hated flying, but when Chris had called about a problem with spring training he had dropped everything and gotten a flight. As people started to collect their things and leave, he turned his phone back on and raised his eyebrows at the number of calls and texts he'd missed. He hustled off the plane with his carry-on bag over one shoulder as he listened to his voice mails.

April. He closed his eyes and groaned. He'd

forgotten about the bike tour when he'd heard Chris's panicked call. He regretted it badly—not calling her after he'd booked his ticket—but he'd been so intent on getting to Arizona that it had slipped his mind. He slowed and dialed April's number. "I'm so sorry. I had to leave town on a moment's notice."

"It's fine."

But the tone of her voice didn't sound like she was fine. It sounded controlled and clipped. "A client called and needed me."

"A client needed you? I see."

Her words and tone reminded him of the fights he'd had with Marissa before the divorce. "Do you?"

"Actually, I'm getting a very clear picture." She paused on the other end. "Goodbye, Zach."

The words sounded so final that they made his chest ache. "Wait, I'm sorry I didn't call, but that's no reason for the two of us to be over so soon."

"Zach, we never got started. Not really. It's better that we end things now rather than drag it out."

"April, let me explain." He couldn't let her

go. Not like this. He needed to try to fix it. "I screwed up, I know. I should have called, but I forgot."

"You wouldn't have forgotten if I was your mom. Or your client."

"That's not true."

She took a deep breath. "I love how you take care of your mom. And I love how you treat your clients with respect and take their needs seriously." She paused. "I love you, Zach, but I can't be with you. I can't be a second thought. Or a third. Or even a fourth."

She loved him? The thought made his heart soar. Made him want to tell everyone who walked by that an amazing woman loved him. But at the same time, he was about to lose her. "April, let's not do this over the phone. Let's think about this, and we can get together when I'm home in a few days. Please wait for me."

"The thing is, I'm done with waiting."

"April…"

"I'm making a point of living and enjoying my life now. Not waiting for the perfect time. Or the perfect guy."

"You know I'm not perfect."

"No, but I thought you might be perfect for me." She paused, then sighed. "Guess I was wrong." It sounded like she was teary. "I wish you all the best."

And then she was gone. He stared at his phone. Tried calling her back, but she refused to answer and it went to voice mail. Someone jostled him, and his carry-on bag fell to the floor. He stooped to pick it up, slung it over his shoulder and found the line of taxis. He'd fix the problem with Chris, then he'd fix his relationship with April.

He knew how to fix things with people because he gave them what they wanted and squelched his own needs. The problem was, April wanted to be without him. And even if he wanted to be with her, he'd give that up to make her happy.

CHAPTER THIRTEEN

APRIL GRABBED ANOTHER tissue from the box and blew her nose. Sherri was rubbing her back while Page scowled from the sofa.

"He doesn't deserve you. I'm going to call him and give him a piece of my mind. No one ditches my best friend," Page all but growled. She propped herself up on her elbow and started to reach for her cell phone.

April hauled Page back to the sofa. "I was the one who broke up with him." This brought a fresh batch of tears, and she plucked another tissue from the box. "Why did I do that?"

Sherri leaned in and April felt Sherri's hand gently guiding her head to Sherri's shoulder. "That is a great question," Sherri said. "I thought you liked him."

"I love him. But he loves his mother. He should. The thing is, she and his clients will always come first. He bends over backward for them. I admire him for it. But where does that leave me?"

Page struggled to sit up. "So let me get this straight. You broke up with him for the same reason that you're in love with him."

"I never said it made sense." She wiped her eyes and blew her nose, discarding the wadded tissue in the pile on the coffee table. "I'm done with putting my life on hold. I'm going for what I want. No more waiting, no more hesitating. I can't, I won't waste one more minute of this life. And if that means I have to let him go, then that's what I have to do."

Sherri ran her hand through April's hair. "If you think it's the right thing to do."

"I refuse to let him treat me like I'm a second thought. That someone else will always come before me. If he loved me…" She wiped her eyes again at the fresh batch of tears. "If he loved me, then—"

"What makes you think he doesn't love you?" Page asked, handing her a fresh box of tissues.

"Do you make plans with someone you love then forget because something more important came up?" April shook her head. "I would have turned my life upside down for him. But that's because I love him. If I mattered to him, he would do the same."

"Dez says that he loves me because it's harder not to." Sherri gave a lopsided smile. "And loving me isn't easy, as he can tell you. I'm tough and independent and stubborn. But he wouldn't forget if we had plans."

April motioned toward Page. "See? Even Dez gets it." She took a deep shuddering breath. "It's fine. I'll concentrate on finishing my list, and I'll find my own happiness." She brought out her journal. "The next thing that I want to do is throw a big party. I'll be cancer-free for a year in two weeks, and I want to celebrate that in the biggest way possible." She turned to her friends. "I was hoping you two could help me plan it?"

Sherri nodded. "Put my madre down for bringing some food. Do you like enchiladas or tamales? Hers are the best."

April flipped to a clean page and wrote that down. "I thought I'd get some ideas from Mrs. Rossi. Maybe something I can make, like a pasta dish."

"From Zach's grandma?" Page raised an

eyebrow at this. "Is that a good idea? She might not like the fact that you broke up with him."

"Good point, but it won't hurt to ask her. And I'm writing her and Mr. Rossi down on the guest list." She made a note. "I got some tips at that wine tasting for what to look for and buy. I'll be sure to have pop and water for the kids." To Sherri, she said, "You'll bring Dez and Marcus, right? And your cousin Mateo, too. Maybe we can have some salsa dancing. And I was going to invite your parents, of course. I appreciate how your mom tried to teach me how to knit. I only wish it had stuck."

"I'm sure they'd be pleased." Sherri smiled warmly.

April turned back to Page. "I'm inviting my whole department, all the doctors, nurses, everybody. Dr. Frazier and Dr. VanGilder. My family, obviously. Who am I forgetting?"

"Where do you plan on having this party? You're talking about a hundred people if they all bring dates," Page pointed out. "Maybe you should pare things down?"

"No way. This is about celebrating the fact

that I stared death in the face, and made it blink. I dreamed of this party when I was too sick to get off the couch like you, Page. I thought about who I wanted to be there and what we would eat and music we'd dance to. I wanted to make sure this is a memorable night." She thought again about the party she'd dreamed up a year ago. "And now I want to make it even bigger and louder and full of so much joy that people will never forget it."

"You're asking a lot from a party," said Page.

"I know." April handed the journal and pen over to her. "And I need you to be there. So write down ideas that you can be a part of. Because I can't imagine a night like this without you."

"What if I'm sick?"

"Then I'll decorate a bucket with streamers and balloons that you can keep next to you." She squeezed Page's shoulder. "I'm not just throwing this party for me. I beat cancer, and I know you can, too."

"You're going to keep bugging me until I agree to go, aren't you?"

April nodded. "And when this is all over, we'll plan your party, Page. And yours, too, Sherri. Because we deserve to celebrate after everything that we went through. We came out the other side alive." She put a hand to her chest. "I may have to live every day with my scars, but they're proof that I'm one strong woman."

Sherri was teary and put her hand over her heart. "Cancer couldn't keep us down." She looked over at Page. "What do you say?"

"Right now, cancer is kicking my behind." Page held her hand out between Sherri and April. "But I'm all in."

April and Sherri put their hands over Page's, and they grinned at each other. This was going to be the most fabulous party ever.

HIS CELL PHONE BUZZED, and Zach reached over the stack of papers on his desk to check it. Not April. Not wanting to talk to anyone else, he put the phone down and returned to marking up the contract for a new client he hoped to sign later that week. The phone chimed, letting him know that he had a voice mail waiting.

Dalvin knocked on his office door and stepped inside. "It's after seven, so I'm going to head out for the night. Do you need anything before I go?"

Seven already? Seems like now that his mom didn't need him at home, he stayed later and arrived earlier. He'd even spent the night on the sofa in his office, once or twice, when he realized that the sun would rise in a few hours. "I'm fine. I was just getting ready to leave myself."

His assistant gave him a look that made him think he didn't believe him. Not that Zach believed it himself. He probably wouldn't have realized the office was empty until the cleaning crew arrived. He rubbed his eyes. "Dalvin, what day is it?"

"Thursday."

Zach swore and looked at his watch. "I was supposed to meet my mom ten minutes ago for a family counseling session. I should have had you put it in my schedule." He grabbed his phone and checked the voice mail. The nursing home reminding him of the appointment.

He swept the stack of papers into a desk

drawer, locked it and ran past his assistant to the elevators. Dalvin joined him before the elevator arrived. "Zach, don't take this the wrong way, but what are you doing?"

He pressed the down button on the elevator a dozen times, knowing it wouldn't make it come up any faster but he did it anyway. "Trying to make it to this appointment. Should I take the stairs?"

Dalvin grabbed the cuff of his sleeve. "You're still spreading yourself too thin between your mom's care and your clients. You're not eating or sleeping. I thought that putting your mom in the nursing home was supposed to make your life easier by dealing with some of the stress. What happened?"

The elevator doors opened, and they stepped inside. Zach pressed the button to take them to the underground garage. He tapped his foot and watched the floor numbers descending on the display. When Dalvin cleared his throat, Zach gave him a shrug. "I don't know. It was supposed to be easier."

"When do you take the time to do something for yourself?"

That was funny, and Zach chuckled at it.

Time for himself? When was that supposed to happen? He kept moving, never resting, because slowing down meant that he wasn't doing what he was supposed to do. He needed to hustle for his clients, for his mother. If he was going to take over the agency from Mike in six months, he needed to push himself, not slow down. He had to make all their lives easier.

He paused. But who was making his life easy? He glanced at Dalvin, who at least made sure that he ate at mealtimes and kept him on track, most of the time. But having his assistant didn't make his life mean something more. Make him happy. He'd been using all his energy on everyone else. And now found himself feeling empty.

"I'll plan something this weekend."

Dalvin clucked and shook his head. "Sad day when you have to plan to take care of yourself."

The elevator doors opened on the garage level, and Zach strode off. He'd think about it later. After the counselor. And after signing that client.

Then maybe he could think about what had gone so wrong with April.

He reached the nursing home and ran up the ramp to the front door. On his drive there, he'd called to say he'd been tied up and was running late. The counselor had been terse, but had accepted his excuse. Seemed like that's all he'd had lately: excuses.

He picked up his visitor's pass from the front desk and sped toward his mother's room. But it stood empty when he arrived. He checked the tiny attached lavatory, but she wasn't there either. He sprinted to the nurses' station farther down the hall. "My mother, Mrs. Harrison, isn't in her room. Has she been taken to the counselor's office?"

The nurse replied, "Dr. Danz is meeting you both in your mother's room."

"Well, she's not there. I just checked." He tried to tamp down his anxiety, but the thought of his mother wandering somewhere made his stomach churn. She was probably searching for him, and he'd put her in this place. It was all his fault. All of it. He'd lost his mother, and he had no one else to blame. "She knew I was coming tonight, right?

We've been talking about it all week. Is there a code you can call to lock down the ward until we find her?"

"I'm sure she's fine. Probably visiting with one of her friends." The nurse glanced up at him. "We'll do a room check."

"She gets confused easily."

"Mr. Harrison, most of my patients are in the same boat, which is why we have the electronic doors to protect them from leaving unattended. We haven't lost her, I promise."

Zach nodded, but he didn't feel confident in the nurse's assessment of the situation. He started walking to each room, calling his mother's name. In the fifth room, he found her sitting in a rocking chair while another patient showed her how to string beads onto a chain. "Mom."

She smiled up at him. "Zach, you're here. Come look and see what I'm making."

"Where were you?"

She glanced around the room. "Right here with my friend." She pointed at the woman and frowned at her after a moment. "What is your name again?"

He rushed forward and leaned down to hug

her. "I thought you were lost. I thought something bad had happened to you."

She chuckled and reached up to pat his cheeks. "You worry too much."

Because he'd had to. He'd worried and stressed and done his best to take care of her. "We should go. We have an appointment with the counselor."

"But I want to stay here and spend time with my friend."

"You can do that after we're finished."

Reluctantly, she handed the half finished necklace to the other woman. "We'll have to do this later. If I can remember where we left off." She gave a wink and laughed at her own joke.

But Zach didn't find it very funny. They checked in at the nurses' station, and one paged the counselor. A young woman with blond curls who reminded him of April approached them with a clipboard. She held her hand out to his mother and then to him. "I'm Dr. Danz, and I thought we'd take tonight's session in your room, Mrs. Harrison. Maybe you can show me how you've settled in."

They proceeded to his mother's room, and

he paused to have the women enter first before following them inside. His mother sat on the bed as Dr. Danz commented on the personal touches before settling in the recliner by the window. "You've really made it homey, Mrs. Harrison. I love the plants."

"Call me Kate."

"How do you like it here so far, Kate?"

His mother scrunched up her face as she considered the question. "I don't know. It's nice sometimes, and I have friends. I like the nurses, they let me watch whatever I want on my TV."

"What don't you like about it?"

"The lime gelatin with pineapple."

She made a face, to which Dr. Danz laughed. "Anything else?"

His mother hesitated. "I haven't seen Robert since I've been here. I miss him."

Dr. Danz nodded and made a notation on her clipboard. "And you, Mr. Harrison? What do you like about your mom staying here?"

He stared at the woman, wondering if she was serious. He didn't like it. He didn't appreciate the fact that his mother had to be confined here. That his thoughts were consumed with whether she was okay, or if he'd get a call asking him to help the staff to calm her. He hated that the house was too quiet when he returned at night, if he did at all. "I don't know."

"Yes, you do. Please share with us what you like about this change."

He let out a breath. "I can't because I don't like it."

Dr. Danz made another note. "Did you hear what your mother said? She's made friends, and besides the lime gelatin, she doesn't mind the food."

"And that's supposed to make it all better? To make her better?" He ran a hand through his hair. "She's still confused. She seems quiet right now, but give her time and she'll lash out at you about more than just a desert. And she's still searching for my dad, who's been dead over twenty years. Is that progress?"

"Zach, why are you so angry?" his mother asked.

He turned to look at her. "I'm not."

She gave him the face he remembered from

his childhood when he'd been caught in a fib. "I like it here. I wish you did, too."

Dr. Danz asked his mother more questions about the facility and the staff, writing down her responses. She also asked what year it was and who was currently president. She recited a list of words and asked his mother to repeat them. After ten minutes, she stood and put a hand on his mother's shoulder. "I'll see you next week, Kate. Thank you for showing me your lovely room." To Zach, she said, "Can we talk outside for a moment?"

He followed after the counselor as if he was a schoolboy in need of a scolding for bad behavior. He probably should have kept his doubts to himself. When the door closed behind them, Dr. Danz peered at him. "Do you know why I have these counseling sessions with the family?"

"To show us the progress my mother has made. Or lack thereof."

"Your mother has other doctors responsible for that. I'm here to show the family that their loved one is in good hands and to address any concerns they may have." She paused and looked at him directly. "The counseling sessions with me are for the sake of the family, not the patient. So tell me. How have you been sleeping?"

What? "Who cares? I'm fine. It's my mother you should be concerned with."

"I'll take that to mean that you're not sleeping. How about eating?"

"I do fine."

She wrote a few lines on her clipboard. "Mr. Harrison, I understand that you want your mother to improve. That you want her memory to return and for everything to be like it was before. And I'm sure that I'm not the first doctor to tell you that the reality is she's probably the best she's going to be. The doctors have her on meds to stabilize her moods, but she's not going to get better."

He bit his lip and took a deep breath. "I know."

"Do you really? Or do you tell yourself that because it's easier than really accepting the awful truth that the mother you knew is never returning?"

"I don't need a psychologist."

"Maybe, maybe not. But until you deal with your guilt, it's going to eat away at you and cause more sleepless nights." She wrote something on a sheet of paper, then tore it off her clipboard. "Here's the name and number of a colleague who specializes in working with caretakers. He was once like you, caring for his aging mother and trying to hold on to her so tightly that he lost everything else."

"I haven't lost anything." But he took the slip of paper and folded it before putting it in his pants pocket.

"We can talk about that next week." She patted his shoulder, turned and disappeared around the corner.

Zach stared at the floor between his feet, contemplating the counselor's words. In truth, because of his mother he'd almost lost his job. He'd lost his mother long ago when the disease had started stealing parts of her away. And now he'd lost April.

He fingered the paper in his pocket. He'd never been one for seeking out therapy, but he could almost hear April's voice in his head. If things weren't working now, what could it hurt to try something new?

APRIL PULLED INTO the parking lot of the strip mall that held the offices for Hope Center and glanced at her passenger. "Are you sure you're up for a meeting tonight?"

With a wan smile, Page gave her a nod. "I need one. It will be good to see some friendly faces. And to get out of the house, if nothing else."

Unsure if this was the best idea for her friend, April nodded and parked the car near the door. "All right. But if you need to leave early, just give me a signal."

"How about I say something like, 'I think we should go now.'"

At least the chemo treatment hadn't robbed Page of her dry sense of humor. "That will work, I guess. But I was hoping for something more like tugging on your ear, or tapping the end of your nose."

"If that will make you happy." She took a deep breath before turning and opening the passenger door.

Page looked pale, ashen. What little hair she had once had was already gone. The hollows in her cheeks had started to show. April had once hoped to never see her friend like this again, but here they were. Facing another cancer diagnosis. She hurried around the car to get to Page's side in case she needed assistance. But if nothing else, her friend's stubborn side won out, and she walked toward the Center without help.

Lynn rushed over to them and gave Page a hug. "What are you doing here? You should be home resting."

"If that's how you greet everyone, no wonder our attendance numbers are down."

"Glad to see chemo hasn't dimmed your sarcasm."

Page rolled her eyes and headed for the circle of chairs. Because of April's insistence that they be early, they were the first to arrive and had their pick of seats. Page chose the comfortable plush armchair and lowered herself into it.

Lynn pulled April to the registration table to get signed in. "How is she really doing?"

"She's taking cancer on for the third time. How would you be doing?" April wrote out name tags for herself and Page and stuck hers to her chest. "But she was determined to come tonight, so I guess there's that."

April took the seat next to Page and handed her the name tag.

Others started to arrive, including Sherri, who exclaimed when she saw Page and ran over to them. "I'm so happy to see you."

Page glanced at April. "That makes at least one who's glad I'm here."

"We're only concerned about your health. Your immune system…"

"I'm fine." Page hugged Sherri, who leaned down to put her arms around her. "Dez could handle being on his own tonight?"

Sherri claimed the seat on the other side of Page. "He and Marcus are having a guys' night with my cousin Mateo. I figured I could use some time with my boob squad."

Page groaned. "We really need a new name."

April laughed along with Sherri as Lynn called for the group's attention. "Tonight, we're going to talk about finding a support system. The cancer journey is not a solitary one. We need to surround ourselves with family and friends who will be there for us. Sometimes we need them to physically take care of our needs. Other times, it's their emotional support that we crave when we have those bad days."

April thought back to the weeks that her mom had come to stay with her, taking time off from work and away from her dad to help her through it. Even now, on the other side of treatment, the memory of her mom washing her hair, cooking her meals and driving her to appointments made her eyes misty. She dabbed at the corner of one eye.

Sherri raised her hand. "My madre was my biggest helper. Still is. But it's because of Page and April's support that I've discovered what true friendship means." She reached over and took Page's hand. "Anything you need, you ask. You were there for me, and I plan on being there for you every step of the way."

Page rolled her eyes again, but a hint of a smile made her lips twitch.

April took Page's other hand. "One of the lessons I've learned through my journey is that we're stronger together. When I am weak, I lean on you. When you need help, I give you a hand. We're here to celebrate the good news and cry when it's not so good. My friend Page is going through a tough time right now, but I know she'll be there with me to celebrate this weekend at my party."

"You'll make me go whether I want to or not."

"But you want to go."

"Only because Sherri's mom is making her tamales."

April smiled at her, then turned to the rest of the group. "You've all been there with me on this journey, so I hope to see you Saturday night at my house."

Page tapped the end of her nose after a half hour, so April made their excuses and they left the meeting early. She drove Page home and got her inside. Page winced as she lowered to the sofa and pulled an afghan over herself. "I'm really considering painting this room when I feel better. I've spent so much time staring at these walls that I can tell it needs some sprucing up."

April couldn't contain the snicker. "Starting your own second-chance list?"

"Don't laugh. Sometimes the words you say do get past my thick skull."

April pressed a kiss to Page's cheek before

leaving. When April got to her car, she didn't start it right away, but thought back to what they'd talked about at the meeting. Page had been one of her major supporters, but there was another she hadn't taken the time to thank. She pulled her cell phone out and called her mom.

"Hi, honey. Is everything okay?"

April bit her lip to stem the tears that threatened. "I know it's later than I usually call, but I wanted to thank you for all you did for me when I was sick."

"You don't have to do that. I'm your mother, so of course I was going to help you."

"But I never said it." She took a deep breath. "Those days after my surgery when it was just the two of us meant a lot to me. I knew that I was going to be okay because my mom wouldn't let anything happen to me. You fed me, bathed me and told me you loved me in a million little ways. Thank you."

Her mother sighed on the other end. "You're welcome, sweetie."

"Love you."

She could hear her mom's smile through the phone. "Love you, too. See you Saturday."

ANOTHER WEEK PASSED, and Zach hadn't found the time to call the counselor or to do something for himself. He'd divided his days between work and visiting his mother. He had to admit that she seemed happier at Sunny Meadows. She had experienced only one meltdown, but the staff had been there to calm her quickly. The staff had called to let him know, assuring him that everything was okay. Not taking their word, he'd driven to the facility to see for himself. He found his mother chatting with a nurse about Zach's days as a baby and showing off pictures in an album. She hadn't needed him. He should have felt relieved.

That Saturday night, he visited his grandmother's house. A free night was rare, but he was still taking care of his responsibilities, rather than simply relaxing or doing something fun. At the front door, Nonna greeted him wearing a bright blue dress and heels, her hair coiffed and looking as if she was heading out on the town. "You're early. Good." She handed him two pans of what smelled like lasagna. "Put those in your car, and I'll check on Frank."

He obeyed her orders and deposited the food in the trunk. It would leave his car smelling of tomatoes and cheese for days, but he didn't mind. He returned to the house and found both grandparents looking spiffy in fancy clothes. Pops eyed his outfit. "You can't go to the party looking like that."

Zach checked his button-down shirt and jeans. "Nonna said she only needed a hand with something."

Nonna thrust a paper bag at him. "We're taking food to a friend's party, and you're going to drop us off and pick us up at eleven." Once they were outside, Nonna shut and locked the door.

"You couldn't drive yourself?" he asked.

She dismissed his suggestion. "We can't drive so well in the dark. And besides, I heard there's going to be some fabulous wine tonight."

Zach shot a look at Pops, who shrugged and moseyed toward the car, opening the front passenger door for Nonna. Zach took a deep breath and followed them. He got into the driver's seat and turned the key in the ignition. "So, where is this party?"

"I'll give you directions," Nonna replied.

By the third turn, he'd figured out that it was April's party. Nonna didn't have any other friends in his neighborhood. He braked at a stop sign and faced his meddling grandmother. "I'm not going in with you."

"You should. You'd be lucky to have that doctor lady." Nonna glanced in the rear window. "Look. The car behind us is going to honk his horn if you don't drive."

"You should be on my side."

"I am. That's why I'm dragging you to this party."

Zach looked at his grandfather in the back seat, who remained silent, but grinned. Zach continued driving to April's house, muttering under his breath about well-meaning but interfering relatives. "I'm doing just fine."

"Are you? Because that's not what I see. You're sleeping at the office. And when you're not there, you're visiting your mother." Nonna shook her head. "Enjoying your life is about finding a balance. It can't all be work or all about your mom. April held out a chance for you to have real happiness, and you let her sit in the rain."

He'd tried to apologize to April, but she hadn't taken his calls. He hadn't meant to forget her or their plans. Something had come up. But even he knew that excuse sounded lame. "I didn't mean to."

"Okay. So now you can make it up to her. Prove to her that you can show up. Or better yet, prove it to yourself. Show up for your own life. You take care of everybody else. It's time you do something for you."

Zach pulled in front of April's house. Cars lined both sides of the street, so he double-parked to let his grandparents out. He grabbed the trays of lasagna from the trunk and carried them up to the house. Nonna knocked on the front door, and Zach's breath caught when it opened. But it wasn't April. Instead, Page smiled at his grandparents, but her grin faded when she saw him standing there. "What are you doing here?"

He held up the food. "Bringing lasagna."

She took the trays from him and motioned at his car. "You might want to move your car. And if you plan on staying, let me give you a word of warning. Tonight is about April. And if you so much as cause her to frown, I will make sure that your life is miserable for years to come."

"I didn't mean to hurt her."

"Well, you did." And she shut the door in his face.

He turned and went to his car. When he got inside, he debated leaving his grandparents there and driving home. He could return later and pick them up when the party was over. He drove to his place and parked in the driveway. The thought of the empty house made his stomach hurt. But that could have been lack of food. He'd eaten breakfast with his mom at the nursing home that morning, but had he eaten lunch?

He got out of the car and started walking the two blocks back to April's house. At least she would have food.

APRIL TOOK THE trays of lasagna from Page and placed them among the other platters. Perla had made her chicken tamales, and Page had brought over a huge salad from their favorite restaurant in Greektown. April's parents arrived with a mouthwatering pot of spicy chili. And another friend from the hospital had samosas. Bags of chips littered the counters along with several dips, and for dessert, April had ordered a cupcake tower from a local bakery as well as a sheet cake in bright pink frosting.

She'd also decorated her home in pink streamers and balloons. It looked like a four-year-old's birthday party, but the sight of the helium balloons bouncing and swaying made her smile.

And that's what the party was all about: the people and things she loved that made her feel joy. Her mom arranged a plate of chocolate–peanut butter cookies on the table and then gave April a hug. "This looks fabulous, sweetie. You've outdone yourself."

"It's not too much?"

Her mom tapped the end of her nose. "It wouldn't be your party if it wasn't."

Music played softly, but she planned on turning it up later when the dancing got going. She'd strung up pink twinkling lights around her deck to create a dance floor and hoped she'd get a chance to salsa with Mateo again. Though the way Page watched him as he moved among the other guests meant she might have to wait her turn.

The doorbell rang, and she walked over to answer it. Her heart stopped for a moment at the sight of Zach standing on the porch. She glanced behind her at Mrs. Rossi, who smiled wickedly before turning back to her conversation with Perla. He had his hands shoved into his front jeans pockets, his head lowered. "My grandmother insisted that I come."

She stepped aside so that he could enter, but he stayed on the porch. "There's food and beverages in the kitchen. You look like you could use something to eat."

"April…"

He raised his head to look at her, and compassion flowed out of her toward him. He might have been dressed nicely, but the dark circles under his eyes and unkempt hair made him look sickly. She put her hand on his shoulder. "What's wrong? You don't look so good. Is it your mom? Is she okay?"

"She's fine." He shook his head, staring into her eyes. "There's something wrong with me, though."

That was obvious. She joined him on the

porch and shut the door behind her. Several friends from work arrived, and she gave them a nod but kept her focus on Zach. "Are you sick?"

"No. Yes. I don't know." He ran a hand through his dark hair, making it stick up worse than it had been. He looked like he was hurting, as if something had gone horribly wrong since the last time she'd seen him. Someone called her name from inside, and she turned toward the sound.

Page opened the front door. "I can't find a serving spoon for one of the pasta salads." She glanced at Zach. "I need her right now. What do you want?"

"This is your party. I don't want to take up your time." Zach moved past them both and entered her house.

April worried. "He looked bad, didn't he? Tired and worn-÷out like I haven't seen him before. I wonder what's going on."

"I thought you weren't going to wait for him."

"That doesn't mean I can't be concerned about him."

"Just don't go falling for him again. He

hurt you once already. He doesn't get a second chance."

April rubbed her best friend's shoulder. "Have I mentioned how happy I am that you came to my party tonight?"

Page rolled her eyes and mumbled something about Miss Mary Sunshine gone wild. Inside, April scanned the living room. It was packed with family and friends. The sight of everyone mingling, talking and laughing brought a smile to her heart, and she touched her chest where the warmth spread down her limbs to her fingers and toes. This was what she had wanted all those months she'd been sick. To be surrounded by love and friendship. To know that she wasn't alone.

The song changed to one of her favorites, a zippy tune that made her want to snap her fingers and shake her hips. She held up her hands and started to do just that.

ZACH STOOD BY the wall in the living room, shifting from one foot to the other. He watched as April started to dance alone. She closed her eyes and gave her entire body up to the song, mouthing the words, a smile flirting around her lips. She looked magnificent.

In her absence, he had floundered and lost his direction. He'd gotten caught up in everyone else, anything to keep his mind occupied. and not allow thoughts of her to intrude. But here in her house, he felt like he could find his way home. That he could live a life of purpose, yes. But one of passion, too. That he could figure out how to have a career, family and love, too.

He shook his head. He really needed to get something to eat before he fell to his knees, weeping. He blamed April for making him feel things, to want things that he hadn't had a chance to pursue before. Page eyed him from the other side of the room, so he nodded to her, but then beat it into the kitchen to get a plate of food.

A tall man stood with his son at the table laden with a variety of dishes, including his grandmother's. The man nodded at him, then turned to his son. "Only take what you can eat, Marcus. I'm sure we can get leftovers from Abuela later."

Zach reached for a plate and started to

move around the table, taking a little bit of each dish. The man snapped his fingers. "I know you, right?"

Zach looked up at him and shrugged. "Uh, maybe. I'm Zach Harrison."

"Ah, the sports agent. That's right. I've heard of you." He held out a hand. "Dez Jackson. I can't wait for Johnson to hit the field with the Lions this fall. This is our year. I can feel it."

They shook hands and returned to filling their plates. "That's the plan."

"You're with April, right? You're one lucky man. She helped my Sherri when she got diagnosed with cancer. I don't know how we would have made it through without her." He smiled wider as a woman entered the kitchen. "And there's the love of my life."

The woman put her arms around his waist and kissed his cheek. "Mateo is going to officially start the dancing in a little bit." She swayed her hips, and Dez mimicked her movements.

"I've been waiting all week to dance with you." He placed a kiss on her lips.

She turned to Zach, and her eyes sparkled

with amusement. "You've got a lot of nerve showing up tonight." She leaned over and dipped her head close to his. "Personally, I think it was brave. Don't let us down."

She and Marcus left the room, and Dez's eyes followed his wife. Zach cleared his throat. "I think you're the lucky man, Dez."

"I am." He winked and left the room to join his wife.

The music's volume rose, and April entered the kitchen. Opening the double doors that led to the backyard, she gave him a glance, then crooked her finger at him. He didn't even think about it, but put his plate of food down and followed her outside.

April held her arms out to him, and he joined her on the deck. Held her hand and twirled her to the rhythm of the song. They came back together, and she smiled up into his face as they moved in sync. The heat of her body warmed him where he touched her. Other couples soon joined them on the deck, but he didn't see anyone but her. Just her.

The song ended. He didn't let go of her hand. Instead, he stood there, looking down into her eyes. "April…"

She put her finger to his lips. "Don't talk. Just dance."

A slow romantic ballad started, and she pulled him into her arms. She rested her forehead against his chest, and they swayed to the lyrics of finding love. But he didn't need the words to know that he'd found it there with her. She'd been next to him during some of the most difficult days of his life. She had encouraged him and supported him. Had loved him through it all. Even waited an hour in the rain because she wanted to be with him.

He didn't deserve her, but a part of him wanted to prove himself worthy even if it took the rest of his life.

He put a hand to the side of her face, and she looked up at him. He glanced around at the other couples, even caught sight of his grandparents dancing a few yards away from him. He tugged her hand, and they walked off the deck toward the back of the yard under a tree that had started to leaf. The music floated on the air toward them, and the smell of the budding flowers made him drunk on her.

He put his hands on both sides of her face. "April, I messed up with you, and I'll probably mess up again. I don't know how to balance my life yet. I get so caught up in everyone else's that I lose sight of my own. But I'm willing to change. For you."

April took his hands away from her face. "No. Don't change for me. Change for you. Because you want it for you. Make your life better for you first." She looked back at her guests, some of whom had stopped dancing to watch them. "That's what my second-chance list is about. Me. And finding happiness for myself so that I can share it with you."

"I love you so much, April. I'll spend every moment proving I'm worthy of you."

"You already have, Zach, you have. You're here, aren't you?"

He pulled her into his arms. "I want to work on my second-chance list."

She kissed him lightly. "Let's work on it together."

He closed his eyes and pressed his forehead against hers. "I knew you were trouble the second you lectured me about my client."

"And I've been determined to make you notice me since you ignored me for your cell phone."

He pulled it out of his pocket and tossed it away. "You're going to turn my world upside down, aren't you?"

She grinned. "That's the plan."

APRIL GRIPPED THE leather cord that tethered her to the metal pole that stretched along the cabin of the plane. Zach stood in front of her, but he'd turned so that he could look at her. She closed her eyes and took several deep breaths, but it still felt as if she couldn't get enough air into her lungs. She was going to pass out if this kept up. "I don't know if I can do this."

"C'mon, Sprader. You promised that you'd help me with my list. What happened to wanting to experience new things?"

"I didn't think you'd want to jump out of a plane!" She opened her eyes and glanced outside. They were so high up. She loved this man standing before her, but she was starting to doubt if she could follow him by hurtling through the sky.

Their instructor called their names and gave them a last-minute pep talk. He finished by sliding the bay door open, and motioned them forward, so they would all jump together.

April strained to see below and shook her head. "No, I can't. Sorry, Zach, but you're asking too much."

"Maybe you're right. I might be asking the wrong question." He dug through his pocket and pulled out a small blue velvet box and opened it to reveal a diamond solitaire. "What if we got married? And we'll make a new second-chance list of things we both want for each other."

April stared openmouthed at the box. "Like a honeymoon in Italy?"

"And a house and a dog and maybe some kids further down the path."

When she was sick, she'd hoped to find a man who would enjoy life with her. And now, there he stood, holding out a diamond ring. "Yes. Yes to all of that."

Zach beamed and slid the ring on her finger. He took her hand in his, then nodded toward the instructor. "What do you say, April? Should we jump?"

"I'm scared."

"I know. But we'll be fine if we do it together."

She held back, but only for a split second. She turned and gave him a quick kiss. "Let's take the plunge."

And they jumped out of the plane, April opening her arms wide to embrace everything that life could bring.

* * * * *

Don't miss Syndi Powell's first
HOPE CENTER *story,*
AFRAID TO LOSE HER, or
her other previous romances
for Harlequin Heartwarming:

THE RELUCTANT BACHELOR
RISK OF FALLING
TWO-PART HARMONY
THE SWEETHEART DEAL

Available from www.Harlequin.com!

Get 2 Free Books,

Plus 2 Free Gifts—

just for trying the Reader Service!

Get 2 Free Books,
Plus 2 Free Gifts—
just for trying the Reader Service!

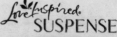

HOME on the RANCH

YES! Please send me the **Home on the Ranch Collection** in Larger Print. This collection begins with 3 FREE books and 2 FREE gifts in the first shipment. Along with my 3 free books, I'll also get the next 4 books from the Home on the Ranch Collection, in LARGER PRINT, which I may either return and owe nothing, or keep for the low price of $5.24 U.S./ $5.89 CDN each plus $2.99 for shipping and handling per shipment*. If I decide to continue, about once a month for 8 months I will get 6 or 7 more books, but will only need to pay for 4. That means 2 or 3 books in every shipment will be FREE! If I decide to keep the entire collection, I'll have paid for only 32 books because 19 books are FREE! I understand that accepting the 3 free books and gifts places me under no obligation to buy anything. I can always return a shipment and cancel at any time. My free books and gifts are mine to keep no matter what I decide.

268 HCN 3760 468 HCN 3760

Name	(PLEASE PRINT)

Address	Apt. #

City	State/Prov.	Zip/Postal Code

Signature (if under 18, a parent or guardian must sign)

Mail to the **Reader Service:**

IN U.S.A.: P.O. Box 1867, Buffalo, NY. 14240-1867
IN CANADA: P.O. Box 609, Fort Erie, Ontario L2A 5X3

* Terms and prices subject to change without notice. Prices do not include applicable taxes. Sales tax applicable in NY. Canadian residents will be charged applicable taxes. This offer is limited to one order per household. All orders subject to approval. Credit or debit balances in a customer's account(s) may be offset by any other outstanding balance owed by or to the customer. Please allow 3 to 4 weeks for delivery. Offer available while quantities last. Offer not available to Quebec residents.

HRCBPA18

Get 2 Free Books,
Plus 2 Free Gifts –
just for
trying the
*Reader
Service!*

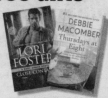

Get 2 Free Books,
<u>Plus</u> 2 Free Gifts—
just for trying the Reader Service!

Get 2 Free Books,

Plus 2 Free Gifts—

just for trying the Reader Service!